WILLOW CREEK SUMMER

BARBARA MCMAHON

Willow Creek Summer

Chapter One

Leigh Gaffney turned onto the wide street and slowed for the long driveway. Ancient oaks lined the avenue, meeting overhead in a lush green canopy. Dappled sunlight spotted the asphalt and the scent of roses filled the air. She turned her car into the drive and headed straight to the back of the house.

Though she had visited Uncle Paul and Aunt Lila every summer from the time she turned ten until her last year of college, she was surprised at the sense of homecoming that filled her. Her visits had only been for the long school breaks while her own parents, both anthropologists, used the months to go abroad to participate in archeological digs.

She'd been back for a few Christmas visits, but the unexpected welcome today warmed her.

The old house looked as familiar as ever, its dark green shutters and pristine white clapboard newly painted that spring, according to Aunt Lila's most recent letter. The wide front porch still carried the comfortable old wicker rockers, though she thought the colorful cushions looked new.

The yard needed work, the grass to be cut, the flower beds weeded. They'd been neglected since her aunt and uncle's departure on their longed-for cruise a couple of weeks ago. Her cousin obviously put off the yard care as long as possible.

It seemed nothing had changed with her cousin. She'd never liked yard work.

Leigh stopped the car near the small back porch. She leaned back in her seat, exhausted. Hoping she had enough energy to make it into the house, she idly contemplated the flagstone walkway. The grass growing between the flat stones needed trimming. Maybe in a couple of days she'd have enough energy to get out the mower and take care of the yard. It'd be a small return for staying in the house while her aunt and uncle were gone.

But in the meantime, she felt as if she could close her eyes and sleep for a week right where she sat.

The key word was energy. And inclination. She sighed. She didn't expect to find either sitting in the car.

Movement to her right caught her attention. Slowly she turned her head. Her aunt's next-door neighbor, Cooper Bryant, strode across the yard, heading in her direction. Tall and well-built, he was barefoot, snug cutoff jeans his only attire. It was obvious from the wet black muscle car and the water running from the hose lying near the vehicle what he'd been doing.

His dark hair looked tousled. The cool mocking gray of his eyes was not yet visible. But she knew what to expect. Her heart lurched, then raced as she stared through the windshield at the approaching man.

As a teenager, she'd had a huge crush on Cooper.

And he'd never once looked her way.

Taking a deep breath of resignation, she withdrew the key and grabbed her overnight case. Time enough later to unpack the car and dream over long-ago days. The things in the small bag would tide her over until morning. After a solid night's sleep, she'd have the energy she needed for the task of unpacking. Or so she hoped.

Climbing out of the car, she stretched and once again

wondered why people rarely used the front door to her aunt's house. It had to do with parking, she supposed. Though visitors were fond enough of sitting on the front porch once they arrived, almost everyone used the back door.

"Leigh?" Cooper asked as he drew close. For a moment his gaze ran from the top of her head to her feet. Then the familiar, mocking smile tilted up the corners of his mouth. "Leigh Gaffney."

Leigh's heart pumped hard against her chest, her hands grew damp and every nerve ending tingled. Just from his look. She swallowed hard and nodded. Had nothing changed in the years since she'd last seen him?

The old, remembered feelings swept through her, tingling and magical. For one second she wished that he'd whisk her into his arms and kiss her like there was no tomorrow. Of course she'd wished that every summer while she was growing up. Wishes that never came true.

"Well, well, little Leigh Elizabeth Gaffney, all grown up. And you did it so well," he drawled, folding his arms across that wide expanse of chest and leaning against the hood of her car. His gaze made a leisurely trek over the feminine curves and valleys of her body. From the glint that appeared, Leigh knew he approved.

Anger flared at his arrogant perusal, his mocking tone. She was in no mood to deal with this. Ignoring the tantalizing expanse of bronze chest, she glared at him, holding her own. All grown up and not about to make a fool of herself over this man ever again.

"Well, well, Cooper Skyler Bryant, still obnoxious as ever," she returned, refusing to be intimidated.

She'd dueled with champs these last few years. She was no longer the shy teenager with a monstrous crush. She could hold her own these days. And it was time her cocky neighbor realized that.

Start as you mean to go on, her aunt had always said.

A glint of appreciation lit his dark eyes as his gaze met hers. Slowly he nodded.

"I try to please."

And she bet he pleased any woman who gained his attention. He was as gorgeous as ever. Thirty-four years old and he still looked good enough to eat. She'd known him over half her life. Had once tried everything she knew to entice him to see her as an available, interested female when she'd been younger. And failed miserably.

The differences in their ages had worked against her. And that bad experience he'd had in college, combined with the example of his own mother, had made him extremely wary around women. Fine for casual dates, Cooper was a perpetual playboy.

Good for as long as he was interested, but commitment had become an anathema to him. Love 'em and leave 'em had been his motto when she'd last seen him and she suspected nothing had changed.

It wasn't fair, she thought, as her gaze wandered over him. Shouldn't he start looking a bit worn around the edges instead of drop-dead gorgeous? He was approaching middle age, after all. Yet his shoulders and muscular chest gleamed in the late afternoon sun, tanned and sleek. Muscles moved when he uncrossed his arms and she noticed he looked as fit as a teenager. His long legs were spread as he leaned arrogantly against her car. Just looking at him made her knees weak.

She sighed, too tired to even muster up a flirtatious smile for the man. What was the point? She recognized lost causes when she saw them. At least recently, she acknowledged. He'd ignored her most of her life. It was past time she gave up any hopes of a relationship between them. He was Cooper, forever unattainable. And she was tired. Very, very tired.

"Here for a visit?" he asked.

"Yes."

"You must need it, you look like something the dog dragged in."

"Gee, thanks, Cooper. I'm always a sucker for honey words. Careful, you'll turn my head."

"I deal in facts."

"Ha, as long as they suit whatever client you're defending. Otherwise, you change them to suit your needs."

Leigh swayed a bit. She needed to get inside.

"Whatever works. And I don't change the facts, though I have been known to suggest a different way to look at them."

He shrugged and tilted his head to better study her.

"What works for me right now is bed. See you around."

Turning, she started for the house.

"Staying long?" Cooper called after her.

She shrugged and kept walking. She was too tired to banter with him today. Too tired after the long drive to do anything but find a bed and crash. Maybe if she slept a week she'd feel better.

The air inside the old house felt fresh and cool. Smiling at the welcome that seemed to seep into her with every step, Leigh wandered through the lower floor to the wide stairs leading to the second story.

It was seven o'clock on a late spring evening. Too tired to even think, she quickly climbed the stairs, entered the room that had always been hers, stripped off her clothes and climbed into bed, grateful to find someone had made it fresh for her arrival. Probably Aunt Lila, or maybe her cousin Meredith. She was too tired to even consider who might have been more likely.

Job burnout. She'd always scoffed at the concept before. But the reality proved all too true. And it was frightening. If she had half a brain, she'd have seen the writing on the wall. But she'd been too busy trying to prove to the world that she was invincible. And it had caught up with her. Big time.

Tomorrow she'd begin to make plans for the future. But not tonight. The trip had been long, boring and endless. She craved oblivion as never before. Even the thought of seeing Cooper again couldn't keep her awake.

In only seconds, she fell sound asleep.

"Good morning, sleepyhead."

A familiar voice woke Leigh the next morning. Opening one eye a slit, she frowned at her cousin standing in the doorway. Meredith had always been cheery in the morning. A trait Leigh did not share.

"Go away."

She pulled the pillow over her head and tried to block out the soft rustling as Meredith moved into the room. She heard the soft clink of china. Even beneath the pillow she could smell the rich aroma of freshly brewed coffee.

Slowly she eased the pillow back a couple of inches and peered out.

"I may forgive you if that's coffee," she grumbled.

Meredith sat on the edge of the bed with a bounce and grinned at her cousin.

"You look like something the cat dragged in. When did you arrive? I expected you to call me. If I hadn't swung by last night I still wouldn't know you're here."

"Last night I was too tired to do anything but sleep. Isn't it awfully early for you to be visiting?"

Leigh gave up thoughts of going back to sleep and pushed herself up against the headboard. She reached for the delicate china cup. Her aunt had a flair for the romantic and all her china was delicate and fragile.

"I waited until ten," Meredith said virtuously.

"It's after ten?"

Leigh hadn't slept that late since college days. She shook her head to clear the cobwebs and then sipped the hot brew.

"Ummm, all's forgiven. This is delicious."

Meredith smiled smugly.

Leigh looked at her cousin and tried to hate her. Meredith was beautiful, always had been and always would be. Her dark glossy hair glowed with health. While Leigh's own mousy hair gained golden highlights in the sun, it now hung in waves around her shoulders in a plain dull brown. She hadn't spent any time in the sun for months.

Where Meredith looked great without a speck of makeup, if Leigh didn't wear mascara on her light eyelashes, they were lost. She did think her own dark chocolate-brown eyes were striking, where Meredith's eyes were a nondescript hazel.

"Are you all right?" Meredith asked, tilting her head as she studied her cousin.

"Just taking inventory. Why are you so darn beautiful and I got stuck with average looks?"

Meredith laughed. It was an old familiar complaint.

"Leigh, you're pretty, you just don't take time to make the most of what you've got. Take your eyes, for instance, they're your best feature. A bit of the right makeup and they'd be the focus of your entire face."

"Yes, I know. Old story. Maybe I'll play around with makeup this trip. We can do dress-ups. So why are you here? Don't you have a job?"

"Of course I have a job. I'm just taking today off. When I stopped last night, Cooper said he'd seen you come in but hadn't seen any sign of life since. I came upstairs looking for you, but you were fast asleep. Tough drive down?"

"It's a long way from New York City to Willow Creek, North Carolina."

"You didn't have to drive it all in a day. If you'd taken your time, it'd have been easier."

"I wanted to get home," Leigh said softly, sipping her coffee.

"I guess. How are you doing, really? I know it couldn't have been easy to give up your job."

"I didn't precisely give it up. When the company was sold, it became a matter of time until most of us lost our jobs. Restructuring is the official term these days."

"But you worked so hard."

"Right. Dumb move on my part. I should have seen no matter what I did, the new company had its own agenda. So the long hours and all the stress didn't pay in the end. I'm so tired now I can hardly think. So since I have more time on my hands than I know what to do with, I decided to take up your mom's offer to visit for a while. Regroup until I decide my next move. I'm due some down time. The new company was generous in their severance money, so I'm not in dire straits. After I rest up, I'll plan for the future. Maybe I'll get a job in Charlotte. Or go back to New York. I have a lot of friends there."

Leigh wasn't sure what she'd do in the future. Right now, it was too much effort to even begin to decide. She felt lonely, adrift as never before.

"You have friends here. And family," Meredith reminded her gently.

"There is that," Leigh acknowledged.

She'd been so excited when she first moved to New York after college. Now the thought of living closer to home—or the only place she considered home—held a huge appeal. Was it backlash or was she due for a change?

"Oh, speaking of family, guess what I found. Wait a minute."

Meredith jumped up and rushed from the room. Ruefully, Leigh reached for a napkin to mop up the spilled coffee. Another trait Meredith had, unbounded energy.

Leigh thought she envied her cousin for that right now more than her looks. She hated the lethargy that seemed to invade every cell. When would she bounce back?

Leigh finished the coffee and snuggled down in the covers. She'd always had enough energy until recently. She'd recoup, it'd just take some time. The thought of doing nothing all day except maybe dabbling at gardening or just lying in the sun, sounded like heaven. And it felt great to be home.

Her parents were in the Aegean this summer. And for the last two years had taught at a university in California. Prior to that they'd done stints at numerous colleges and universities across the country.

She wondered how the only child of nomads could so strongly yearn for a permanent home and roots. Often she felt closer to her mother's sister than her own parents.

"Look what I found when Mom and I cleaned out the attic a couple of months ago. It's hilarious."

Meredith held out a leather-bound journal.

"I haven't read that much, but what I did was funny."

Leigh took the book and brushed her fingers across the cover. The rich leather felt soft and supple, though it looked old.

"What is it?"

"Great-grandmother Megan's diary. She started it the day she turned eighteen. The journal was a birthday gift from her father. And Mom said she wrote in it up to the birth of her first baby, great-uncle Lloyd. You have to read it. She has a recipe for getting the right man for a perfect marriage."

"A *recipe* for getting a man?"

"Yes, how to entice a man, how to get his interest and hold it. It's so funny and old-fashioned. You can read it while you rest up. I bet it cheers you up. Then I'll read it again. Do you remember her?"

"Vaguely. She died when I was ten. The year I first started coming here for summer vacation. Wasn't she old?"

"She sure seemed to be, I think she was in her mid-nineties when she died. This book is almost an antique."

"How much did you read?"

Leigh asked, turning to the first page, fascinated. Her great-grandmother Megan had written this, a bit of family history that she never expected to see. Megan had beautiful handwriting, clear and perfectly formed.

Leigh began to read the first paragraph.

"Read it when you're alone. I'm here to visit,"

Meredith took it from her cousin.

"I've only read the half. Mom got first dibs. She finished it before they left. I'm sacrificing my turn to let you have it while you lie around. What do you want to do today? I thought we could go to the country club for lunch. They have a wonderful salad bar during the week. Maybe lie by the pool for a while. I want to do lots of fun things on my day off."

She slipped the journal onto the table beside the bed.

"Sounds fine with me," Leigh said, glad to have someone else take charge for a change. She'd been living on her own for so long, it was nice to be cosseted.

"I think I'm in love," Meredith said abruptly.

"Again?" Leigh said, unsurprised.

Her cousin was in love with someone new every time she saw her. And it usually lasted a month or two and then she'd move on. Did she fear commitment? Maybe there was something in the water.

Cooper Bryant never committed to a woman. Willow Creek, North Carolina, appeared on the outside to be the perfect rendition of a friendly southern town. Yet her cousin was twenty-nine, same age as Leigh, and she hadn't found the right man yet.

Of course, Leigh thought ruefully, neither had she. But she had a reason. Not that she would ever tell anyone that Cooper had spoiled her for other men. She used him as the measure for everyone she dated. So far, no one else came close.

"Who's the lucky man this time?" Leigh asked pushing back the sheet to get up.

She crossed to her carryall and began looking in it for something to wear until she unloaded the car.

"He's a friend of Cooper's, actually. Moved here on Cooper's recommendation. His name is Josiah Collins, and he's the newest vet in town."

"Vet? An army vet?"

"Veterinarian."

Leigh paused and turned to stare at her cousin.

"Veterinarian? Meredith, you don't even like animals."

"That's what he does. *I* don't have to do anything with animals. But I'm really interested in him as a man. He's fun to be with and doesn't talk shop."

"How old?"

"He knew Cooper in college, so he's about the same age."

"Never married?"

Meredith shook her head.

"What does that have to do with anything? You and I have

never been married either."

"But we're still in our twenties."

"Right, for a few more months," Meredith said dryly.

"The point is that we're still young, Cooper's thirty-four."

"And that's old? It's only five years older than we are."

"We both know Cooper has no interest in getting married."

She paused a moment, remembering his scathing laughter when she'd shyly shared girlish dreams with him one summer. The humiliation ran deep at the time.

"We both know why Cooper's in his mid-thirties and still unmarried. But what's kept this Josiah from forming some lasting commitment before now?"

"Good grief, Leigh, how should I know? Maybe he was waiting for me. Just because a man isn't married by a certain age doesn't mean he won't ever marry. Not every man is as cynical as Cooper. Besides, who knows, maybe one day the right woman will come along and find a way to get around even Cooper's defenses."

Leigh looked out the window. At one time she fervently wished she'd be that woman. But she'd grown up. And the events of the past few months firmly showed her the error of tilting against windmills! She'd learned to stop beating her head against an immovable barrier. Practical would become her new watchword.

She looked at Meredith and smiled.

"I'm happy for you, Meredith. When can I meet him?"

Mollified, Meredith bounced up.

"This weekend for sure. I'll have you both over for dinner or we can go out or something. Hurry and get dressed, there's lots to do today. I have to make the most of my time. I'm not normally a lady of leisure like you, remember?"

It was late afternoon by the time Meredith dropped Leigh

back at home. Lunch at the country club had been pleasant. Leigh spoke with a couple of friends from the past who wanted to know how long she'd be visiting and they made plans to get together.

Meredith had then dragged her to the new mall, to show off the stores, and urged Leigh to get a few new things.

Shopping with her cousin could wear anyone out, Leigh thought as she waved at the departing car, though Meredith's intent had been to cheer her up with new clothes. Smiling, she headed for the house. It had worked. The two sundresses she'd bought were totally unlike the business suits she'd worn for the last seven years. She loved New York, but it hadn't taken a day to fall back into the slower rhythm of Willow Creek. Was she a chameleon that changed colors to suit her background, only in her case changing lifestyles to suit her locale? She liked the slower pace. It suited her own state of mind right now.

"Leigh?" Cooper called.

She turned. What was it about Cooper Bryant that threw her into such turmoil? She'd met and dated handsome men in New York, successful, dynamic. Yet none of them had set her nerves on end, dampened her palms and interfered with her breathing.

Cooper looked as if he'd just come from his office. The light gray suit was formal, nothing like the cutoffs of yesterday. His white shirt and silver tie emphasized the deepness of his tan. It was early June and he already had a tan. She felt anemic next to him. A few days by the pool would change that.

"Hi, Cooper," she said calmly, belying the involuntary butterflies dancing in her stomach. It wouldn't hurt to look, she told herself, as her eyes feasted on the man. His tie was loosened and his shirt unbuttoned at the top. She liked him better in cutoffs, she thought irreverently, though the style of his suit showed off his broad shoulders, his tall lean frame. His gray eyes seemed to peer right into the heart of her and she dropped her gaze lest some lingering foolishness showed.

She hoped he wasn't remembering that summer.

"You ran off pretty quick last night," he said when he reached her.

"I was tired. It was a long drive."

She didn't have to answer to him. She'd long ago given up on the man, so she saw no point in wasting time. Frankly, she didn't have the energy yet to join in some verbal sparring and come out ahead—or even hold her own.

He reached out and gently traced the skin beneath her eyes with a fingertip.

"You look a bit better today, but still tired. Tough few months?"

"I've had better."

Even when his hand slid into his pocket, she felt the lingering impression of his touch. Swallowing hard, she reminded herself she wasn't interested in the man.

Not, not, not, she chanted inside, wishing she could believe it.

There was no point in submitting herself to dreams that something would come of his neighborly greeting. He and his brother and father had lived next door to her aunt and uncle for years. When his father retired to Florida, Cooper had bought the home and continued to live in it. Her Aunt Lila kept her fully informed of the doings in Willow Creek.

Except for his years at college and law school, the house next door had been Cooper's home all his life. He had the roots she'd longed for.

However, it wasn't roots that caused her awareness of the man. It was his own presence, his dark good looks, his eyes that seemed to see down into her soul. His humor had enchanted her as a younger woman, his arrogance and self-assurance appeared so glamorous to someone who had felt shy, uncertain and out of place for much of her childhood.

When she'd been younger, Leigh had flirted for all she was worth in an effort to make him interested. First she'd been too young. He'd treated her casually, like a younger sister.

Then when she'd grown up, Cooper had changed and become cynical and bitter and took no pains to hide the fact from her or anyone else.

"Finally tired of New York?" he asked, his gaze moving across her face.

He'd seen the shadows beneath her eyes. Did he also see the weight she'd lost?

"Tired, in any event. I'm here on vacation. Maybe I'll see you around."

She smiled politely and turned back to the house. She'd taken a dozen steps when he spoke again.

"If you need anything, call me."

She turned around and began walking backwards.

"Thanks, Cooper, but Meredith's nearby. And it's not as if I don't know my way around."

He stood with his hands in the pocket of his trousers, his gaze steady. Again she noticed how his starched white shirt contrasted with the deep bronze of his tan. How much time had he spent outdoors this spring? A successful attorney should be too busy to have a lot of time to spend idly in the sun.

She wondered how his practice fared. She knew he was formidable in the courtroom. When he'd first started, she'd attended a court session to see him in action. The intervening years had honed his skills, she felt certain. Though even in the early days, he'd been dynamic.

"You haven't been here for a while. Things change," he called.

"I've made a few visits. I was here two Christmases ago," she said, glancing over her shoulder. The front porch stood only six feet away. She knew the door would be unlocked. No one locked up in Willow Creek.

"And before that it was a couple of years, I believe."

He took a step toward her, as if to close the distance between them.

She smiled involuntarily. He sounded as if he were cross-examining a witness. How accurate did she have to get?

"That's right. I really have to go, Cooper. These packages are getting heavy. See you."

She turned and ran lightly up the front steps and into the house.

Cooper watched Leigh skip up the steps to the porch. For an instant he stared after her. Something was wrong. He couldn't put his finger on it, but it nagged at him.

Suddenly, he realized what it was, what had changed. Leigh made no attempt to flirt with him. All the years he'd known her, she'd flirted for all she was worth. As a teenager, she'd hung around and had done all she could to test her new-found femininity on him. Even while she'd been in college she'd tried to get his attention.

He hadn't seen her in years. Where had he been Christmas two years ago?

And what had caused the change? Her smiles seemed polite, yet her manner had been decidedly un-Leigh-like. Distant, disinterested. Had she finally gotten over her crush on him?

Her persistence had been embarrassing when he'd been younger. Then amusing during his college days. Finally annoying.

He'd told her so, if he remembered correctly. Obviously he had convinced her.

He'd had no time for starry-eyed teenagers bent on a grand love affair. He didn't plan to repeat the mistakes of his father. His mother hadn't stuck around, leaving instead for the glamor and excitement of New Orleans. And after Celia, he'd begun to view all women with a jaundiced eye. Maybe his father was right, women couldn't be trusted. A man was better off on his own.

Still, for years nothing had diminished Leigh's determination. Until now.

Not that he *wanted* her to have a crush on him or flirt with him every time they met. There was no future in it for either of them. But oddly he felt something was missing with her lack of interest. Had he gotten so used to her devotion he now expected it?

What had she been doing these past years? Lila Porter had mentioned at one point that Leigh worked in an advertising firm as a project manager or something. He wondered if she enjoyed living in New York,

She looked exhausted.

He turned toward his house, anxious to change out of the hot clothes he'd worn to work. How long did Leigh plan to visit? Not the entire summer as when she was a child, he felt sure. Long enough for him to see her a couple of times? Hear about life in New York? She'd be his neighbor as long as she was in town, might as well do the right thing.

Cooper walked back to his place, curious about his temporary neighbor. Maybe it was nothing more than Leigh had finally grown up. Maybe now their relationship would evolve into a comfortable neighborly friendship like he enjoyed with her cousin Meredith.

Cooper snagged his briefcase from the front seat of his car and headed inside to change. It was hot for early June. The humidity level rose steadily each day and he knew the summer would arrive in full scorching force before long. In the past he'd have known it was summer by Leigh's arrival.

He didn't remember much about the summers he'd been in college. Of course falling for Celia had taken his mind off everything else. To find out she'd lied about everything, had used him for her own means had cut deep. That discovery caused his vow that entanglements with women were thereafter forbidden. Casual dates set his limit.

But sometimes in the dark of midnight he wondered if he really wanted to spend his entire life alone. Would he ever get lonely enough that he'd chance a more permanent relationship? Find a woman he could tolerate enough to have children with?

He thought he might like to have some kids. He wondered if his brother ever thought about getting married. Nieces or nephews might satisfy these odd thoughts about children.

After changing into comfortable chino slacks and a cotton polo shirt, Cooper went back downstairs. His house was built similarly to the one next door. Both were two stories tall, with high ceilings and large rooms. He'd made few changes since his father moved south.

The comfortable and sturdy furniture had been there as long as he remembered, acquired for comfort rather than for esthetic beauty. Solid upholstered furniture his father had chosen when his wife had run away and never returned.

There was nothing in the house to show his mother had ever lived there. For a moment Cooper tried to picture some of the furnishings that had been around when he'd been very small. Only a hard, cherry wood chair came to mind.

Cooper didn't remember much about his mother. His brother, Samuel did, but at three years older than Cooper, he'd been ten when their mother left.

Mrs. Norris came once a week to vacuum and dust. The rest of the time he was on his own. Which was the way he liked it.

He pulled a beer from the refrigerator and looked out the window. He could see into the Porters' backyard. It was empty. Was Leigh cooking dinner? Had she made plans for the weekend?

He'd further satisfy his curiosity by spending a little time with her. Maybe invite her to dinner at the barbecue place on Route 201 which would offer her down home food she probably hadn't had in New York. And the atmosphere was casual. Nothing she could read into dinner together.

Though she didn't seem to be reading anything in his direction.

Giving in to instincts, Cooper reached for the phone. The number of the house phone next door had been in service since Paul and Lila first bought the house thirty years ago. Cooper didn't need to look it up.

Leigh answered on the second ring.

"Hi, Leigh. Thought we could get dinner together on Saturday," he said easily, leaning against the counter in the kitchen.

He knew there was a danger she'd immediately assume he was interested. But he could deal with that. He genuinely wanted to catch up.

"Sorry, Cooper. I'm already busy. Thanks anyway."

Startled, he realized he'd expected her to leap at the opportunity. Another indication of the change in her attitude. Was that a trace of disappointment he felt?

"No problem. How about Friday?"

"Tomorrow?"

"Yes."

"Nope, sorry, already going out to dinner. Maybe some other time. Oops, I have to go, the timer just went off. Bye."

He looked at the phone before he replaced it.

"A bit cocky in our old age, aren't we, Cooper?" he said aloud. "Thinking she'd jump at the chance to go out with you."

If he needed further proof that she no longer had that teenage crush, he'd just received it.

Suddenly, his interest rose. One of the facets of becoming a successful lawyer was questioning things until he understood every aspect. Leigh's behavior was totally at odds with what he'd come to expect from her. Intrigued, he wanted to know why. And find out a bit more about what she was doing with her life.

Perseverance was another trait of a successful attorney. He'd try again. She couldn't have booked every night of her entire visit. She'd just arrived yesterday. How many evenings had she already committed? Tomorrow he'd call again, and nail down a day.

The clock on the mantel chimed nine when Leigh went to bed. Still feeling tired and a bit listless, she succumbed to an early night. Her day with Meredith had done a lot to raise her spirits and she felt some of her enthusiasm return when she glanced at the journal still resting on the bedside table.

Slipping beneath the covers, she reached for the book, opening it with a sense of adventure that'd been long missing. In only seconds she became totally engrossed in the scenes unfolding between the pages.

Her great-grandmother had painted a very detailed picture of her life, of her parents and brothers and sisters. The descriptions were enthralling and Leigh felt as if she were meeting each of these ancestors in person.

Then the tone changed. Megan had written:

Turning eighteen is a milestone. Sometime soon I will have to find a husband and settle down to the life for which I was raised. Patricia Blaine has already become engaged and she is but seventeen. I know my future husband is out there, but it may be up to me to find him. I've asked my mother and aunts about this, wanting to do the best I can for myself. And they've given advice, some contradictory, some old-fashioned. But from everything I've heard, I have decided to devise a plan for finding the perfect mate for a perfect marriage.

"Well, Great-grandma Megan, I hope it's a good plan. I could use one myself. If you think eighteen's old, what would you have thought about twenty-nine and unwed? And with no man even on the horizon," Leigh muttered as she turned the page.

The first thing to always remember is that a man likes to do the chasing—just make sure not to run so fast he can't catch you. An occasional glance in his direction would be acceptable, I believe, but in this wild and open time demure and shy are strong lures. I'd never be so bold as to brazenly speak first to a man, or show by my demeanor that I was interested in him. He needs to be the hunter, so Aunt Thomasina said. Though most of the men around here no longer hunt, it must be a trait from the Colonial days when hunting was necessary for survival. I'll be the quiet prey and let the man chase after me. Showing casual interest should work. I wonder if Frederick has noticed me. I could walk past him at church on Sunday and make sure I don't acknowledge him until he notices me. Would it work?

Leigh skimmed the next few pages until she came to the entry for Sunday. Avidly caught up in the story of her grandmother's plotting, she was anxious to see the result of the first aspect of her plan.

She'd never known her great-grandfather and couldn't remember his name. She'd only met great-grandma Megan once long ago. Madison had been her maiden name but what had her married surname been? Her mother's grandmother, Leigh wasn't sure she'd ever heard her great-grandmother's full name. Did her plan succeed or fail with Frederick?

Frederick spoke to me after church. I didn't tarry, told him I had to get home to help Mother with the Sunday dinner. I wasn't rude, I'd never display unmannered behavior, but I kept walking and seemed distracted. It was all I could do to refrain from laughing. He followed me all the way to the walkway of our house. It was the first time he'd paid any attention to me. Maybe Aunt Thomasina was right. I need to let him chase me. The key is to make sure I don't move faster than he does.

Leigh laughed softly. How different things were today. If her great-grandmother thought the first half of the twentieth century were wild, she'd have a conniption in today's society.

Then a sudden thought sparked.

Cooper had come after her today when she'd made no effort to seek him out.

For a moment Leigh stared off into space, replaying that afternoon's encounter in her mind. She'd been tired and wanted to put down her packages.

She'd definitely not been in the mood to linger and chat. Even when he continued talking to her, she'd been walking away. The first time she'd ever done that with him.

And for the first time since she'd known him, he'd pursued.

Even calling later to invite her out to dinner. She'd said no. That should have ended things, but now she wondered.

She picked up the journal and reread the passage. Was there a grain of truth in Megan's plan for finding a perfect mate?

Maybe she'd see what happened if she played hard to get.

She was so glad Meredith had left the journal with her. Reading it would give her something to do. She had nothing else planned over the next few weeks.

For a moment she wished she could see into the future. Would following Megan's advice cause a change in the way Cooper saw her?

She smiled, switched off the light and lay in the dark, planning how to play hard to get with a man who normally acted as if she didn't exist. Tonight had shown a definite sign he'd noticed her.

Would remaining aloof have any effect on the future?

What could it hurt? she wondered just before sleep claimed her. Tomorrow she'd put the plan into action and observe the results. It'd be a campaign of a kind, similar to her ad campaigns. Nothing was decided with one layout. There were several needed to ascertain if the overall plan had a chance of success. Now how could she test this premise?

Chapter Two

When Leigh awoke the next morning, she felt refreshed for the first time in months. Smiling as she dressed, she glanced at the journal resting on the bedside table. How silly she'd been last night. As if following Megan's ideas would insure a happy marriage with the man of her dreams.

She must have been more fatigued than she suspected. To think ignoring Cooper would make him interested in her. Ha! She'd been ignoring him for years while she lived in New York. She hadn't seen any signs he even noticed she was gone.

When Leigh went down to prepare breakfast, it was already mid morning. She couldn't believe how much sleep her body craved. A direct result of all the long hours she'd put in over the last months, she knew. But for the first time in weeks, she felt rested and ready for anything. Maybe she'd tackle the yard.

During the day Leigh mowed, trimmed and weeded. Wearing skimpy shorts and a halter top, she added some color to her skin as well while doing the yard work. Shortly before noon she pulled on a light yellow cotton shirt with short sleeves to protect her shoulders. She didn't want to burn.

It felt good to be doing physical labor in the hot sun. Her mind wandered, skipping on topics, drifting in and out of daydreams.

By mid afternoon, she finished. The lawn looked as if a gardener had taken pains with it. The grass was evenly mowed, edges trimmed. The flower beds had been weeded and deadheaded and now the colorful blossoms flourished.

Satisfied with a job well done, she made a pitcher of lemonade and took it into the backyard, pouring herself a large glass. Gratefully, she sank onto a recliner beneath one of the old oak trees. The shade felt good. She had yet to shower and get ready to go with Meredith and Josiah to dinner at the Fibbing Fisherman Café, a local restaurant.

But she had time to spare and deserved the break, actually *needed* a break after all the work she'd done. It was a good kind of tired, however. Not like what she'd experienced in New York.

When Cooper's sleek black car pulled into his driveway two minutes later, Leigh went still. She suddenly remembering the journal entries and advice written by great-grandma Megan. Sipping her cool lemonade, she wondered if she dare try to ignore the man. He hadn't pursued anyone that she knew of since he'd been in college.

Would her acting distant pique his interest?

More likely it would make him happy to be left alone.

He climbed out of the car, briefcase in hand. Taking work home on the weekend's not worth it, she thought cynically. She'd done that for months and her reward had been the loss of her job.

Looking away from Cooper, she frowned, wishing she'd known before what she'd learned over the last year. She'd have enjoyed life more and left the work to those who were now in charge of the company.

"If you're going to be there for a few minutes, I'll change and join you," Cooper called when he spotted Leigh.

She looked at him, her heart skipping a beat. His dark hair

looked as if he'd run his fingers through it. The business suit fit as if it had been made exclusively for him and the fine tailoring emphasized his height and enhanced his air of confidence and success. Even at the end of the day, he looked as fresh and sharp as early morning. She wondered if he'd been in court today. If so, she bet every female witness lost her train of thought just looking at him.

Leigh nodded once, then lay back, studying the puffy clouds drifting by, trying to remember all Megan had written in her journal. She felt flutters of interest. Try as she might, there was no denying she'd once been attracted to Cooper Bryant and probably always would have lingering feelings for him.

Saying she wanted nothing further to do with him was a lie. But she wouldn't let herself get caught up in some impossible fantasy that they'd fall in love and live happily ever after. She knew better than that.

Still, it couldn't hurt to see how far his new interest would go. Not that she believed her own lack of response sparked his. He probably felt an obligation to watch out for his neighbors' guest while they were away.

Cooper crossed the yard ten minutes later, his eyes fixed on the woman lying in the recliner. He'd changed into shorts and a cotton T-shirt. If she planned to sit out in the hot afternoon sun, he wanted to dress as cool as decency allowed.

Approaching Leigh, his gaze traced over her. Her bare legs were bent at the knees, the shorts almost indecently short. Her skin looked supple and silky, her legs curvy and sleek. The shirt she wore appeared grass-stained. Obviously she'd been working in the yard. A glance at the smoothly cut grass and pile of weeds near the shed provided further evidence.

Her hair was tousled and a hint of pink highlighted her

cheeks. She'd matured, yet her expression still displayed a certain innocence that belied the experiences she must have gained living in Manhattan. With color in her cheeks, she looked downright pretty.

He'd never noticed how much before.

When she heard him, she turned and smiled. Cooper felt it to his toes. He never hesitated in his stride, but the shock of that flicker of physical awareness surprised him. Had he been too long without a woman? Or was there something different about Leigh?

"I made lemonade if you want some," she said casually. "But you need to get your own glass from the kitchen. I'm not moving."

"Or I can share yours," Cooper said easily, pulling the second lounger close to hers and sitting on the edge.

When her eyes widened at his comment, he smiled. He still didn't know what was going on, but he intended to find out.

"You've had a busy day," he said, boldly reaching out to take her glass from her hand. "The yard looks good."

His fingers touched hers. She yanked back, then tried casually to brush her hair away from her cheek, as if not sure what to do with her hand.

Maybe she wasn't as sophisticated as he suspected. Refilling the cold lemonade in the glass, he drank.

"Good—it's not too sweet. You make it from scratch?"

"Yes." She looked at him, her gaze wary. "It's been a long time. How have you been?"

He almost laughed. She sounded like a properly brought up little Southern girl.

"As ever. You?"

"Fine."

"Meredith said you plan to stay for a while," he said, refilling the glass and holding it out to her.

"A few weeks, anyway. Time to regroup, plan for the future. And catch up on sleep."

It looked as if life in New York had been hard on her. Though she looked better today than when she'd arrived.

Cooper noted when she took the glass, she made sure she didn't touch him. Interesting. How far could he push her, he wondered, a hint of mischief rising. She'd bedeviled him as a teenager. Maybe it was time to return the favor.

"Then?" he asked.

"I don't know. I'm considering my options."

She took a sip of the cold beverage as if stalling. He'd interviewed enough witnesses to know a stall when he saw it.

"I thought you went to New York to spread your wings and set the world on fire."

His gaze trailed down her, noticing the softly feminine form hidden beneath the yellow top, her slim waist, her long legs that beckoned. Was her skin warm from the sun, would it feel as silky beneath his fingers as it looked?

"I did. But I didn't realize that I could get my wings singed."

"Meaning the job isn't all it's cracked up to be?" he asked, his gaze sharp.

"There isn't a job at all anymore. There was a takeover."

"Tough break."

"Are you still the up-and-coming hotshot lawyer in Charlotte?" she asked.

"I have my practice there."

"Ever cautious. You sound like a lawyer. I bet you do extraordinarily well at it."

"I keep plugging away. What are you doing for dinner tonight?" he asked abruptly.

"Going out like I said."

"With whom?"

It came out more sharply than he intended.

"Not that it's any of your business, but Meredith."

He relaxed marginally. She'd turned down his invitation in favor of dinner with her cousin. He could understand that. After all, they'd been close as girls and Leigh had been away for a while. They probably had a lot of catching up to do.

"And tomorrow?"

"What is this, an interrogation? I'm not a witness for anything."

"Just curious. You arrived on Wednesday evening. I didn't know you could make so many arrangements that quickly."

"There're probably one or two things about me you don't know," she murmured. "We never were what you'd call close friends, were we? And we haven't seen each other for years."

"Tomorrow night?" he persisted.

"Don't you ever give up? I have a date with Karl Fleming. We ran into each other at the country club yesterday and he invited me out to talk over old times."

Cooper frowned and settled back on the chair, one knee raised. He rested a forearm on it as he studied the trees growing in the back of the Porters' yard. Karl Fleming was closer in age to Leigh. They'd played tennis a lot, as he recalled, when she'd come for the summers.

He'd played with them one time, an arrogant college kid challenging the two young high-schoolers. They'd whipped the pants off him. Of course two to one had been high odds, ones he hadn't challenged again.

"How about Sunday afternoon?" Cooper asked. "We could play some tennis."

"Maybe."

He looked over at her lazily. Her eyes were closed. She balanced the full glass on her stomach, her hands on either side of it. Studying her, he liked what he saw. She wore her brown hair long enough to brush her shoulders. One summer it had been down to her waist. The next year she'd cut it short. He liked this length.

When her eyes flicked open they stared into his, the warm chocolate color soft and mysterious. Her lashes were gold-tipped. Cooper wondered how long it would be before she tried one of her flirtatious blinks he remembered from when she was younger.

She didn't blink. And her wide, innocent gaze had him thinking thoughts best left for the dark of night. She was the crazy girl who had driven him wild several summers with her pestering and flirtation. He'd be the crazy one this time if he gave in to the lascivious thoughts that had begun to build.

"If not tennis, we could drive down by the river, go swimming or something. End up at the country club. They have a nice buffet during the weekend," he said.

He wanted a commitment from her to spend some time with him. The thought surprised him. Normally he didn't push. If a woman said no, he figured it was her loss.

Leigh stared at him for another moment, then looked away, shrugging slightly.

"I'll check with Meredith, but I think I can fit in an afternoon. I'll let you know if it doesn't work out."

Cooper smiled slowly. It took more perseverance than he'd expected, but he knew she'd say yes eventually.

"Maybe next weekend?" she asked.

"What?"

The smile left his face. She was stalling for another week?

"I have plans for this Sunday, but would love to see the river if the following Sunday works for you."

"What do you have going on this Sunday?"

She smiled, flashing amusement in her dark eyes.

"Are you acting *in loco parentis* for Aunt Lila this summer? You sound just like she used to when I was fourteen and thought I was all grown up."

He shook his head, his eyes narrowing. "Just curiosity."

"You need to watch that, Cooper. Tell me about your law practice. Still doing courtroom cases?"

He nodded.

"Come by one day. I'm scheduled for court all week."

"I went to see you once, years ago."

"I remember. You and Meredith snuck in the back and giggled the entire time."

"We did not. Giggle, I mean. I thought you were—"

She grinned ruefully and shrugged.

"I thought you were as good as Perry Mason."

She checked her watch and sat up, sliding her long legs over the edge of her chair, between the two of them. Cooper lowered his own feet to the ground, his knee almost brushing against hers.

"Going somewhere?" he asked.

"I have to get ready for tonight," she said, her eyes watching him warily.

He made no move to give her room. He was so close he could feel the heat from her body, could smell the sweet scent that emanated from her skin mingle with that of the fresh cut grass. Rising languidly, he reached down a hand to pull her up, his palm absorbing the feel of her softer one.

Cooper stood several inches taller than Leigh. Not so much it would give him a backache to kiss her. Where had that random thought come from? He did his share of dating, but for the most part had to know a woman pretty well before having any interest of that nature.

"Skip dinner with Meredith. Have it with me," he said, to his own surprise.

"I can't do that. I said I'd go to meet Josiah."

"And that's important?" He didn't like the spark of jealousy that flared. "Josiah's just another guy."

"Ummm."

She took a breath and glanced to the side, to see if there were room to pass, probably.

"Well, I'll have to see, won't I? Meredith especially wants me to meet him."

"You could invite me to join you."

He slid his hand up her arm, his fingertips caressing her silky skin. Was she this soft all over? His fingers brushed against the cuff of her sleeve, slid beneath the cotton.

"It's not my dinner invitation," she said, her voice breathless.

Cooper felt a certain satisfaction that this odd attraction didn't appear to be all on his side.

"If you're planning to visit for a few weeks, you'll have plenty of time to meet Josiah. Have dinner with me," he coaxed.

She swayed, biting down on her lower lip. Cooper tracked the action, suddenly wanting to be the one to gently bite that soft flesh, then soothe any sting. His gaze rose to lock with hers.

"I can't," she said firmly.

He grasped her other arm with his hand and drew her closer still.

"You can do anything you want, Leigh."

Slowly his thumbs traced random patterns against her skin. Her eyes glazed slightly. Her chest rose and fell swiftly, as her breath caught then released. A few more minutes and she'd capitulate. He knew how to read the signs and she was broadcasting her indecision so clearly a first-year law student could pick up the signals.

Leaning forward, Cooper slowly moved his hands from her arms to her shoulders, then to the delicate column of her neck. Tilting her head back, his thumbs brushed against her jaw. He wanted to kiss her. He wanted to feel the warmth beneath his fingers flare into heat, to taste the tempting lips that seemed to be waiting for his touch. He wanted—

"Are you trying to lead the witness?" she asked breathlessly.

Cooper smiled, liking the sound of her voice. Bemused, breathless.

"That might be unethical," he murmured.

A scant inch from those tantalizing lips, he covered the distance in an instant. For a moment he felt her surprise, then she relaxed and leaned into him.

And poured the rest of the ice-cold lemonade down his leg.

"Blast it!"

He jerked back, tried to avoid the cold sticky liquid. The edge of the recliner caught him behind his knees and he fell in a sprawl half on, half off, the lounger.

"Oh, I'm so sorry. I forgot I had the glass in my hand. Are you all right?"

Leigh set the glass down on the table and stepped closer.

"I don't have any napkins out here. I can run inside and get something."

Trying to hide her amusement, she watched him. Leigh wasn't sure dumping lemonade on a man was considered hard-to-get, but she'd soon find out. Was that diary bewitching her?

"Don't bother."

He rose, slicking some of the lemonade from his leg. His

shorts were sopping wet on the left side. His skin felt sticky.

Leigh stared at Cooper, trying to force some sincerity into her voice.

"I'm sorry, it was an accident."

A bubble of impishness rose. She tried to keep from smiling and giving herself away. Did he think because she had a crush on him years ago, she still did?

"I'm sure it was. If I thought for a moment it had been deliberate, I'd dump the rest of the pitcher on you," he said, looking with disgust at the wet shorts.

When he glanced up at her face, his own expression changed.

"You can make it up by having dinner with me tonight."

She frowned, all thoughts of laughing gone.

"Good grief, don't you ever give up? No way. I told Meredith I'd go out with her and I'm sticking to that. Honestly, Cooper, if you and I made plans would you want me to back out?"

"Meredith's your cousin, she wouldn't care."

"Doesn't matter, I'm not changing my mind."

Leigh drew herself up to her full five feet six inches. There was a principle here, and she was sticking to it—diary or not.

He nodded in acceptance. Unexpectedly his hand shot out and gripped her neck, gently pulling her up against the length of his hard body. His mouth lost its tentativeness, his kiss this time was hot. She opened in response and he deepened the. His mouth moved against hers. For endless moments, time seemed to stand still while the earth spun.

Feelings exploded in Leigh. Surprise was instantly swamped by the hot surge of desire that coursed through. She wanted more, but before she could formulate any kind of thought, he pulled back.

"Maybe you won't break your other dates, but at least you can think about me during them," Cooper said.

He brushed his lips once more across hers then turned and walked across the grass toward his house.

Stunned, Leigh stood and stared after him. In all the years she'd known him, he'd never kissed her before. She'd tried it once and he'd firmly put her in her place. He'd laughed at her, teased her before. But never kissed her.

And what a kiss.

The first attempt had been gentle, an exploration of a kind. But the second had been frankly and blatantly sexual. His mouth had been exciting. And, blast him, it may have spoiled her for anyone else. She ran her tongue over her lips, tasting him. It had been too quick. And she didn't like his reasons for kissing her. Narrowing her eyes, she glared after him.

"Arrogant creature! The last thing I need is any involvement with someone who has no use for women beyond a few casual dates," she chastised herself as she gathered the empty glass and the pitcher.

How typically conceited of the man, to expect her to think of him while out with someone else. And now she probably would.

Heading for the house, she tried to convince herself that the attraction she felt for Cooper was purely physical. It had nothing to do with love or future or even mutual respect. She remembered his scathing comments from years ago. They'd been burned into her mind. He had no use for fatuous teenagers or women in general. He'd made that clear at the time.

Yet something seemed to have changed. She wasn't sure what. Why had he come on to her? Usually he ran as fast as he could in the other direction. He'd really pushed her for a date. And hadn't taken no very gracefully.

She wasn't sure she knew what he was up to, but for a brief

moment it had been gratifying. And, darn it, he was probably right—she *would* think about him tonight.

While taking her shower, Leigh wondered if there was any truth to the steps her great-grandmother had listed in her journal. It seemed preposterous on the surface, but she couldn't deny Cooper had paid attention to her for the first time when she had made up her mind to stay away from him.

Even the lemonade had not dampened his enthusiasm. She grimaced at the awful pun and shut off the water. She'd have to give the idea some serious thought.

Dinner proved to be a lively affair. Josiah was funny and entertaining and seemed delighted to include Leigh on his date with Meredith. At tall as Cooper, Josiah was a bit stockier, and had sandy-colored hair. His sports coat fit nicely, but he didn't exude the same elegance and arrogance that Cooper did.

He also didn't seem to pay any special attention toward her cousin, while Meredith all but devoured him with her eyes. Leigh wondered if Meredith's feelings were reciprocated. And if so, how long before Meredith grew tired of Josiah and moved on to another man?

Leigh had worn one of her new sundresses and liked the softly feminine feeling it gave her. She laughed at Josiah's stories and shared smiles with her cousin when they recounted some of their wilder escapades as teenagers.

When Meredith excused herself after dinner to use the ladies' room, Josiah turned to Leigh with a teasing smile.

"I've heard about you before, you know," he said.

"You have?"

"From Cooper Bryant."

"Oh."

Color flushed her cheeks as mention of Cooper brought

memory of their last encounter—and his kiss. She swallowed hard. She refused to give in to that particular memory.

"Cooper talked to you about me?"

"It was while we were in college."

"Oh. Well, don't believe everything you heard back then," she said, laughing.

She could imagine what Cooper had to say a decade ago.

"He'd come back from holidays or summer vacation and complain about this bratty kid who hung around and wouldn't leave him alone."

"Ouch. I had such a crush on him when I was younger."

She was over that, she assured herself. It'd been a normal teenage crush, that's all.

"So he said." Josiah chuckled. "I sometimes wondered if he didn't secretly like it, though, for all his complaining. You were certainly steadfast. I knew him for the last three years at college and he talked about you a lot."

"I bet."

Leigh took a long drink of her iced tea, then looked at Josiah in consideration. Here was a man who had known Cooper in college.

"Did you know the girl Cooper fell for?"

Josiah's expression grew serious as he nodded slowly.

"Celia Zimmerman."

Leigh hadn't known her full name.

"What was she like? What happened between them?"

"Maybe you should ask Cooper."

"Maybe I should, but you know he won't tell anyone a thing. Was he really in love with her?"

Josiah shrugged. "He thought so at the time."

"And she didn't love him?"

"She pretended for a while. Turns out it was an elaborate hoax to get back at the man she'd once been engaged to. I think Cooper thought he'd found the pot at the end of the rainbow, only it turned out to be fool's gold. As soon as her former fiancé showed up, she dumped Cooper in a public and humiliating manner. Almost viciously, I always thought. And for no reason, except I guess to prove to her fiancé that she really was through with Cooper."

Leigh's heart ached for the younger man Cooper had been. It'd probably taken a lot of faith for him to open up to a woman after seeing his mother desert her family. To have that woman trample on his feelings would have been crushing. No wonder he was so cynical about the whole female gender. She sighed, wishing things had been easier for the man.

Would it have made a difference to how he saw her? Probably not. But her heart ached for the lonely boy she'd known.

"Leigh, did you give away all my deep dark secrets while I was gone?" Meredith asked gaily, rejoining them.

She smiled brightly at Josiah.

"I didn't know you had any to give away," Leigh said observing her cousin's flirtation with the handsome veterinarian.

Josiah didn't seem particularly bowled over to be at the receiving end.

"What were you talking about?" Meredith persisted.

"Cooper, actually," Leigh replied.

"Cooper Bryant? What about him?"

"Nothing much. You said Josiah knew him in college. We were just chatting."

"Cooper mentioned Leigh a time or two," Josiah added.

"I bet he did more than mention her," Meredith said shrewdly, narrowing her gaze at Leigh. "She was forever following him around, pestering him to death, wanting to make him her boyfriend."

Leigh felt the heat steal into her cheeks.

"Thanks, cousin, I defend you and you throw me to the wolves."

"Well, it was true. I never saw what you saw in him. He's so much older than you and didn't seem to care a bit about girls. Until he fell for that one at college. Must not have amounted to much, he dumped her and never hooked up with anyone else on a long term basis. And not for lack of women trying. I've had more friends ask to be introduced to him at various functions around here over the last five years than I can count."

"So did you introduce them?" Leigh asked.

It was hard to remember her own disinterest in the man when her cousin brought up such a tantalizing piece of information.

"Sure, for all the good it does anyone. Sometimes he takes a woman out for a couple of dates, then never calls again. Other times, he never even invited them out for a first date. A lost cause."

"Did you know his mother?" Josiah asked, glancing at Meredith then Leigh.

"No, she left when I was around two. And that was years before Leigh started coming to stay the summers. I've heard my mother talk about it, though. She said it hit Adam, Cooper's father, really hard. As well as the two little boys. They ended up getting a double dose. First they lost their mother, then Adam became lonely and bitter. Never made an effort to find another wife. So Samuel and Cooper constantly heard how awful their mother was with no balancing to soften the recriminations. No wonder Cooper can't trust a woman enough to fall in love."

Leigh met Josiah's gaze, knowing he was thinking about Celia—as she herself was.

"I've got room for dessert," Meredith said brightly. "How about you, Josiah?"

It was after ten when Josiah and Meredith dropped Leigh at the house. She invited them in for coffee, but Meredith declined. Leigh smiled. She knew Meredith had had enough of family. She wanted Josiah to herself for a little while before the night ended.

Waiting by the door while the car drove away, Leigh caught a glimpse of movement coming from Cooper's backyard. Was he outside? Waiting to see when she came home? Unlikely. There was no reason for him to take any interest in her life.

Turning quickly, she let herself into the dark house. She wasn't up to another confrontation with her sexy neighbor tonight. She needed distance and some perspective before she was ready to see him again.

Time to decide how she would handle the memory of that hot kiss they'd shared.

And time to come up with a way to guard her wayward heart. She knew playing with Cooper would be dangerous. After losing her job, and her enthusiasm for her career, she dare not risk her emotional state as well.

Taking the journal when she got into bed, she settled against the pillows. This was more fun than worrying about how to deal with a man. Or her own turbulent emotions.

Don't accept an invitation at the last minute. Make sure he thinks you are busy and have to make an extra effort to spend time with him. This is from Aunt Caroline. But it does go with Aunt Thomasina's advice of being unavailable. Pretend you have other plans, even if it is only washing your hair. And if you truly have another date, let him know others find you appealing as well. Men like to pursue women who are also pursued by others.

Gazing off into space, Leigh nodded. It made sense. But it was not earth-shattering news. Still, hadn't Cooper pushed for a date once she'd refused? And especially after she'd told him she was seeing Karl. Interesting. Was there more to this business than she first thought?

She could pretend she was too busy to see him—if he asked again. And make it seem as if she were doing him a favor to squeeze him in.

Laughing softly at a situation that'd never arise, she began to read again.

Chapter Three

Leigh reread the words, frowning as they blurred. She was tired, probably should have been asleep hours ago, but was too fascinated to give up even a few moments with her great-grandmother's journal. Megan was writing about her mother's admonitions to dress appropriately to her age and gender rather than trying out the new trousers that were the rage.

Mama is shocked with the girls in town wearing the trousers everywhere. She said if the good Lord had wanted women to wear pants he would never have invented dresses. I think trousers look chic, but Mama won't hear of me wearing them. I have to do something to compete for Frederick's attention. I think I'll see about making a couple of new dresses. Lacy, frilly, ultra-feminine. If I can't be on the leading edge of fashion, maybe I'll become known for my femininity. Maybe that will make Frederick feel more masculine.

Leigh chuckled and lay the book on the bedside table. She wanted to know if Megan's ultra-femininity succeeded in making Frederick feel more masculine. She hoped the answer would be in subsequent pages. But it'd have to wait for another time.

Snuggling down against the pillows, she flicked off the light. How different things were in the early half of the previous century when people found trousers for women shocking.

Leigh smiled again. She wore pants all the time, at work and at play. Sometimes she went weeks without wearing a skirt or dress. Wouldn't Megan's mama be totally shocked.

Just before sleep claimed her, Leigh wondered if wearing feminine clothes really had an impact on the males of the species.

"I'm going bonkers," Leigh said to herself the next morning.

Sipping her coffee, she scanned the local paper for any sales. Somehow during the night she'd decided to try Megan's idea about dressing ultra-femininely.

Today she planned to look for some more dresses beyond the two she bought Wednesday, something feminine, yet comfortable. She was on vacation. A time to splurge.

Though she had to watch her money since her source of income was temporarily interrupted. Fortunately, she had plenty in savings to tide her over. And a few more sundresses wouldn't cost a mint. Maybe she'd buy something this afternoon to wear when she went out with Karl.

Though it wasn't Karl she was thinking about, it was Cooper. Darn that kiss.

"Practical," she said firmly. "There is no future in that direction, no matter how much I once wished there were."

She'd had a second lesson in working so hard to keep her position only to lose it. Trying for the impossible plain didn't work.

Folding the paper, she went upstairs to get dressed. It wouldn't hurt to consider what Cooper might like. He was a man, after all. She could at least keep him in the back of her mind when choosing new clothes.

By the time Karl rang the doorbell that evening, Leigh had dithered back and forth a dozen times about her dress and her hair. She'd called Meredith to join her on yet another shopping expedition. When Meredith heard what her cousin planned, she burst out laughing, then joined in with unbounded enthusiasm.

Questioning her in detail about her intent, Meredith commented that Leigh had obviously seen a lot more in that journal than Meredith had when she'd glanced through it.

The result of the day was four more new dresses, some new makeup and a new hairstyle.

Now Karl Fleming was at the door and Leigh wasn'ot at all sure she'd done the right thing. Maybe she should have stuck with her regular clothes. Once she found a new job, these dresses would be relegated to the back of her closet, totally unsuitable for career work.

Still, she liked how she looked and felt in the dress. The scooped neck displayed her neck and shoulders nicely, and the light tan she'd acquired while doing yard work made her look fit and healthy. The fitted bodice revealed her slim figure. The flared skirt moved as she walked, in what she hoped was feminine allure. The soft pink went well with her coloring.

Her hair had been cut and layered and the natural wave brought out. Washed with a highlighting rinse, it sparkled and shone in the light. Framing her face, brushing her shoulders, it looked almost sexy.

Taking Meredith's advice, she'd splurged on makeup to enhance her eyes. Satisfied she looked her best, she was pleased with the day's purchases.

"Hi, Karl," Leigh greeted him when she opened the door.

He was tall, with wide shoulders and a shock of blond hair. His cheerful grin, however, did nothing to raise her blood pressure. She smiled and stepped out, shutting the door behind her.

Why couldn't she be attracted to Karl? She'd known him since they were teenagers. Had enjoyed spending time with him during her summer visits, yet there'd never been a spark of physical attraction between them. They were truly friends and nothing more.

Not that she'd found that spark with any of her dates in New York, either. The only man who once caused sparks was totally off limits. It was way past time she got over Cooper Bryant and concentrated on finding something special with someone else.

"Karl, good to see you," Cooper said, standing on the sidewalk beside Karl's car. He looked at Leigh as they walked down the flagstones, his eyes narrowing as his gaze scanned her from head to toe.

"Leigh," he said easily.

The glitter in his eyes had her heart racing.

"Hi, Cooper."

She felt guilty, like a child caught with a cookie after being told not to have one. Swallowing hard, Leigh took a deep breath. She had *nothing* to feel guilty about. She was entitled to go out on dates. And she'd already told Cooper about tonight.

Thinking about the journal, she thought maybe it was a good thing Cooper saw her leaving. Just because *he* had never wanted her didn't mean other men didn't. If only she didn't feel so awkward.

"How're things, Cooper?"

Karl reached out to shake hands.

"Can't complain. You?"

"Couldn't be better. Business is hopping. We'll be expanding soon and taking in some more help."

Karl was in partnership with his father at the local hardware store. Cooper had spent many hours there as a child. His father loved hardware stores.

Leigh wondered if Cooper shared that trait with his dad.

"Out for dinner?" Cooper asked, his eyes now on Leigh.

The spark of attraction threatened to flare into something larger, but she smiled and stepped closer to Karl, nodding. As if he didn't know.

Karl opened the car door for her.

"I ran into Leigh at lunch the other day. We're going to try that new place in town, Tarheel Tavern."

"Have fun," Cooper said.

"Bye," Leigh said, conscious of his gaze on her all the while as she got into the car.

She felt it as Karl pulled away. Once out of sight, Leigh sighed softly and turned to her date. She had to get over any lingering feelings for Cooper Bryant. Karl was a perfectly nice man and had been kind to invite her out. She'd devote all of her attention to him during the evening.

When Leigh climbed into bed four hours later, she felt exhausted. Picking up the journal, she opened it, wondering if she could keep her eyes open. She'd read just two pages.

The evening had stretched longer than she'd expected. Karl had caught her up about the family business and what he'd been doing since she'd last spent the summer in Willow Creek. Then they spoke about friends. Karl had been a wealth of knowledge of those of their classmates who had remained in Willow Creek.

The closeness she'd once felt as they played tennis and hung out at the country club seemed to have rekindled with no effort. It had been a pleasant evening. And she'd agreed to a tennis date next weekend.

The phone rang.

Instantly Leigh forgot her fatigue. Calls in the middle of the night usually meant trouble. She flung off the covers and ran for the hall phone.

She hoped there wasn't something wrong with her parents.

Or Aunt Lila and Uncle Paul. Surely they'd call her cell. Maybe they forgot the time change and were calling to—

"Hello?" she said breathlessly.

"Did you have a nice dinner?"

"Cooper?"

Sagging with relief, she slowly sank down to the carpet, leaning against the wall.

"Do you know it's almost midnight?"

"Yes, you just got home. Seems like a long time for dinner. How much do you eat?"

"How do you know I just got home? Are you spying on me?"

"Of course not. I saw Karl's car, that's all."

"You just happened to be looking out the window?" she asked skeptically.

"I heard the car and being a conscientious neighbor, I checked."

"Umm, neighborhood watch is alive and well in Willow Creek."

"Have fun?"

"Yes I did," she said defiantly.

Even if she hadn't, she wouldn't admit it.

"I liked your dress. I don't think I've ever seen you in one before."

Leigh smiled at the compliment. She hadn't thought he'd notice, not when he had given a good impression of being more interested in talking to Karl than to her.

"Of course you've seen me in a dress before. I used to wear them to church."

"The last time was years ago, and as I recall, it was not soft and feminine, but tailored and rather intimidating."

"That was a long time ago."

She couldn't imagine anything or anyone intimidating Cooper, especially not a woman. But she was surprised to be remembered the sophisticated outfit she used to wear exclusively.

"So your wardrobe is chock-full of frilly dresses? You surprise me, Leigh."

She opened her mouth to tell him she'd just bought the dress, then snapped it shut. Slowly an idea glimmered. Cooper didn't know her. It'd been years since she'd followed him around like a puppy. She'd grown up and moved away. That made her a stranger to him, for all their shared youth.

"I like feminine dresses," she said slowly.

She was glad she'd read that passage in Megan's journal. She'd felt deliciously feminine all evening.

"Oh, I'm not complaining, honey. Not a bit. You looked good in it."

Honey?

She caught her breath. He'd never called her honey before.

"Change your mind about going out with me tomorrow?" he asked.

Make sure he thinks you are busy and are making an extra effort to spend time with him, had been her great-grandmother's advice.

But Leigh *wanted* to spend the day with Cooper. She was taking careful care of herself to recover from burnout. And part of that was indulging herself in things she wanted. Sacrifices were fine in their place, but she'd sacrificed enough for now.

"I'll have to see," she hedged.

"About what?"

"I have other things to do."

"Like?"

"I'm not on the witness stand, Cooper. Don't interrogate me."

He chuckled.

"I'll back off if you say yes to tomorrow. We can go down by the river, then have dinner at the country club. There's dancing on the terrace, and they have a Sunday buffet that's well worth going for."

"Ummm. Okay, you've convinced me. If I can change my plans, I'll go."

"It's about time you said yes. I'd hate to see you on a witness stand. You'd put everything back weeks."

"Just because I had things to do—"

"Nothing as important as spending the afternoon with me."

"Ha!"

She wrinkled her nose and stuck her tongue out at the phone. Still as arrogant as ever, she thought, warmed by the fact he hadn't changed as much as she might have thought.

"Get to bed. You've been up late two nights. I thought you were tired from New York."

"What are you, my watchdog? I can stay up as late as I want. And just how do you know I was up late last night?"

"I saw your light when I went to bed. I imagined you all tucked up safely in bed. And I have to tell you I think your dress today radically changed my concept of you."

"Oh?"

Was that good?

"I figured you as a no-nonsense kind of New York business woman. One who wore tailored suits. And a cotton T-shirt to bed. Now I suspect there is an entirely different side to you. What do you wear to bed, silk and satin? Lace and ruffles? Is your bed piled high with fancy pillows and frilly sheets?"

She glanced down at the serviceable cotton T-shirt she usually slept in. How long since she had bought feminine and frilly sleepwear? She remembered feeling so glamorous in the long diaphanous gowns she'd worn when she'd been a teen. Daydreams had filled her mind, and she'd spent hours finding just the perfect gown for her allowance.

"Leigh?"

"I think discussing my sleeping attire is a bit personal, don't you Cooper? After all we hardly know each other," she stalled, wishing she had on some lacy confection that would have men drooling if they ever saw it.

Wishing she had the kind of body that caused men to drool.

Sighing softly, she acknowledged wishing never got her anything. Look at her wishes for Cooper. Her wishes for her job.

"Hardly know each other? How can you say that? You've plagued me for years, trailing after me everywhere I went. Have you forgotten your protestation of undying love?" he asked.

She closed her eyes in embarrassment.

"It's totally unnecessary for you to remind me of my childish infatuation," she said slowly. "I was a kid, who had a foolish crush on you. Times change. I have to go now. Goodbye."

Leigh hung up the phone and leaned her head against the wall. She refused to remember that last awful scene when she'd told Cooper she loved him, would always love him.

He'd been mad as a bee-stung dog in those days, at her, at the world. He'd laughed harshly and told her to leave him the heck alone and take her stupid childish infatuation somewhere else. He had better things to do than put up with some goofy teenager who didn't know the meaning of the word, much less the emotion. And forever was a long time. She'd forget him before she was twenty.

That had been eleven years ago. Leigh thought she'd forgotten how awful she'd felt, but at his words the old sensations flooded. She'd been so hurt at his laughter, vowing eternal revenge.

Instead, she'd grown up and moved on in her life. She didn't need him to remind her now.

The phone rang.

Glaring at it, she ignored it and rose. Going into the bedroom, she switched off the light and climbed into bed. She'd read more of the journal tomorrow. Tonight she was going to sleep and forget all about Cooper Bryant and the attraction she'd once felt for him.

Wasn't *practical* her new mantra? How practical would it be to continue to see him, to try out her grandmother's plan? The man was a hopeless case and she'd do well to remember that. She didn't need any more grief. Finding a new job, deciding where to live, she had enough on her plate.

The silence that echoed in the house when the phone stopped ringing was a welcome relief. But it was a long time before Leigh slept.

Cooper slammed down the receiver. He couldn't believe she hung up on him and then wouldn't answer the phone. Pacing to the window, he looked over to the house next door. The light in her room was out. He had half a mind to storm over there and pound on her door until she let him in. He'd intended to tease her about her crush on him, not make her mad.

He sighed and rubbed the back of his neck. He shouldn't have brought it up. Especially since nothing since he'd seen her earlier this week indicated she felt the same anymore.

And that was part of the problem. If he were honest with himself, as he always tried to be, he'd admit he missed her devotion, her wide-eyed worship.

Tomorrow he'd make sure she stuck to her promise to spend

the afternoon with him. If she could arrange to see Karl after being in town only three days, she could darn well make time to see him!

At least she and Karl hadn't taken long in saying good-night. Though they were late enough if they had gone merely for dinner. Had there been more?

He didn't think Leigh was the type to do more with some guy on a first date, but then what did he know? He hadn't seen her in years. And even then it had been brief glimpses as she came and went at the Porters' place.

She was all grown up now, and a woman on her own. Eleven years had passed since she'd tried to kiss him, make him believe she loved him.

Was he still trying to hold on to that? She'd moved on. She dated other men, kissed them, maybe more.

His gut tightened at the thought of Leigh and Karl kissing. He remembered the taste of her when he'd kissed her in the yard. He didn't want another man touching her like that.

And why not?

Not liking the trend of his thoughts, Cooper headed for the shower. Leigh was her own person. She could do what she wanted with her life. But tomorrow he'd make sure she spent the day with him! That would banish all images of her with Karl Fleming.

And if she wanted kisses, Cooper would see she got all she could handle.

"How did the date with Karl go?" Meredith asked as Leigh slipped into her car when she stopped by to pick Leigh up for church the next morning.

"Fine. We had fun and caught up. We might play some tennis next week."

Leigh tried to put some enthusiasm in her voice. The evening had been pleasant enough. It sure beat sitting home by herself.

"Karl's always loved tennis. I remember you two were evenly matched at one time."

"That was ages ago and I haven't played since I moved to New York. I'm sure I'm as rusty as can be."

"Maybe it's like riding a bike, you never forget. I like that dress."

"Do you think it's all right for church? Not too casual?" Leigh asked.

The dress was cool and comfortable. The light blue top was elasticized, hugging her curves like a second skin. The bodice could have stayed in place without the straps over her shoulders. The cream colored skirt with scattered blue flowers moved with her as she walked, the fullness caressing her bare legs, soft cotton against silky skin. Sitting in the car, it covered her knees and pooled around her like a cloud.

"I think it looks lovely. I like the blue sandals with it."

"And I like the comfort. It's just what I wanted."

"So do you feel ultra-feminine now? What else did you read in Megan's journal last night?"

"I didn't read last night. I got home too late. Karl took me to that ice cream parlor near the new mall for dessert and we talked forever."

Leigh left it at that. No sense in telling Meredith about Cooper's call. It wasn't important.

When Meredith parked in the lot by the huge red brick First Baptist Church, Leigh looked around. She recognized many of the people standing in groups, chatting before the service began.

"There's Josiah," Meredith said quietly, reaching for her purse. "Oh, interesting, he's talking with Cooper. It's been a while since Cooper's come to church. I wonder why today?"

Meredith glanced speculatively at Leigh as she shut the car door.

Leigh's heart sped up, despite her efforts to appear cool and collected. This was not what she needed, to run into Cooper after hanging up on him last night. She should have mentioned it to Meredith. If Cooper said anything, her cousin would wonder instantly why she hadn't said something.

Reluctantly she followed Meredith toward the two men, both dressed casually. The sun glinted on Cooper's hair, its rich darkness almost blue black beneath the hot rays. Next to Cooper, Josiah didn't look quite as big as he had at dinner the other night. Both men turned when Meredith called out a greeting.

"Good morning, Meredith, Leigh."

Cooper's voice was low, almost intimate when they joined the small group. His eyes danced in amusement.

"Sleep well?"

"Hi Cooper, Josiah."

Leigh ignored the question and tried to walk by.

Cooper's hand shot out and reached for her hand, effectively stopping her. Slowly he drew her beside him.

"Are we still on for this afternoon?" he asked.

"What are you doing this afternoon?" Meredith asked, looking charming in a yellow sundress with a white short sleeve jacket.

Her eyes darted suspiciously between Cooper and Leigh.

"We're going down to the river, then dinner at the country club."

Leigh shrugged, trying to appear casual.

"Sounds like fun. You didn't mention that in the car."

Meredith turned to her cousin, her eyes narrowed slightly.

Leigh shrugged again, conscious of Cooper's touch. His palm

seemed to burn into hers, the tingles rushing through making it next to impossible to think, much less come up with a coherent reason to give her cousin. She tugged against his hold, but Cooper firmed up his grip.

"Nothing's definite. I have to see if I can rearrange things," Leigh muttered.

"You said yes on the phone last night," Cooper reminded her softly.

"After your last crack, I don't think—"

"We should go in," Meredith interrupted.

"Good idea."

Cooper laced his fingers with hers.

"I don't need you to hold my hand," she snapped, tugging free.

Leigh resented his taking charge. She was aware of the covert glances given them, especially from some of the women who probably had tried to capture Cooper's attention and failed.

Eleven years ago, seven, even five, Leigh would have been thrilled with the attention Cooper paid. But she knew it meant nothing. She refused to let herself be caught up in dreams and schemes again. Life threw hard lessons, sometimes, but it was up to her to learn from them.

No more dreaming? A voice inside questioned. What about trying the steps in Megan's plan for finding a happy marriage partner?

Leigh quelled the internal voice. Trying one or two suggestions didn't mean she was scheming to capture Cooper's undying love and devotion. It was merely a practice run for when she found a man with whom she wanted to build a future. If it worked with cynical Cooper, it would work with the man of her dreams.

"I'll take Leigh home," Cooper said to Meredith at the end of the service. "Save you the trip."

"Thanks, I'd appreciate that."

Leigh frowned at Meredith. What was she, unwanted freight? She could have driven herself to church this morning. Meredith had volunteered to pick her up.

"Don't do anything I wouldn't do," Meredith said gaily as she turned back to Josiah.

"She's going to smother him, if she's not careful," Cooper said as he turned Leigh toward his black car and started walking.

"She likes him. Why not be honest about it?" Leigh said in defense.

"And sometimes I think he likes her. But she comes on too strong. And we both know Meredith has no staying power. She'll burn out soon and flit along to the next man."

"Maybe this time it's for real," Leigh said just for the sake of arguing.

She agreed with Cooper's assessment of her cousin, but had no intentions of telling him so.

"Yeah, and maybe pigs fly."

Cooper reached out to open the door for Leigh.

She slid into the car and tried to muster some argument against Cooper's allegations. She came up with none. Meredith had a track record of falling in and out of love as often as some people changed their socks.

Yet she couldn't let it alone. When he got into the car, she turned to him.

"You view her through cynical eyes. Meredith's a wonderful woman, and will make someone a good wife."

"How long do you think she'll last the course? She can't even stay engaged for longer than six months."

"Just because your mother left your father doesn't mean every woman walks out of a marriage."

"Enough do."

His tone cooled.

"I suppose you see a lot of that in your work."

"No, I'm not into family law. But I have colleagues who discuss it."

"Oh and fathers don't leave?" she asked.

"They do. Marriage as a whole is outdated and overrated. And the leading cause of divorce."

"I can't believe you said that! It's a wonderful institution. We need marriages to keep our society strong."

He looked at her.

"If it's so great, why aren't you married?"

She closed her mouth and turned to look out the window. There was no way she'd reveal how her foolish childish infatuation had influenced her. No other man measured up to her ideal since Cooper. Wouldn't he roar with laughter if he knew?

"I'm busy getting a career started," she said after a moment.

"Then you plan to get hitched?"

He started the car and pulled out on to the street, turning for home.

"Maybe. If I find the right man."

"And how do you *find* the right man?"

"Find isn't the word. Connect with, maybe."

She frowned. It was a good question. She certainly hadn't connected with anyone in New York. Were her standards too high? Or had she just been spoiled by the man beside her?

"Fall in love."

Sarcasm laced his tone.

"Cynic," she murmured.

"Idealist."

"I'd rather be idealistic than cynical."

"I prefer to think of myself as realistic," Cooper said smoothly.

"Not every marriage ends in divorce. Look at my parents or my aunt and uncle."

"Lucky. And it isn't over yet. There's still time."

"You're impossible."

He pulled into his driveway and turned off the engine.

"Do you need to change?"

"Do you think I need to?"

"You look fine just the way you are."

One finger traced the soft skin on her shoulder.

Leigh shrugged away from his touch, a moment of panic threatening. She was out of her mind to think she could spend the afternoon with him and not find herself in deep trouble. His lightest touch about drove her crazy. And he'd mentioned dancing at the country club that night. Could she stand to be held in his arms, swaying her body with his to soft sultry music? Could she do that and not give away her heart?

"I'll be right back."

Trying to calm her nerves, she recalled the passages from Megan's journal. Had she attended the same church where Megan had flirted with Frederick? She'd have to ask her cousin. Or wait for Aunt Lila to get back and ask her what she knew about Megan. Had Megan practiced her ideas on others in addition to Frederick or was he the original test case?

Leigh wondered if she ought to do that, practice before going in for the real thing. She could practice on Cooper. She knew he'd never seriously entertain the notion of marriage. She could try the different suggestions from the journal and see what worked and what didn't. Then she'd be ready to seriously attract her perfect mate when she was ready to settle down.

Speaking of which, she needed to get busy looking for another job. The three days' rest had already buoyed her spirits. The listlessness and lethargy were fading. In fact, she brimmed with ideas and energy.

Unfortunately they all seemed centered around Cooper.

Maybe she'd seriously consider looking for a position in Charlotte. It'd be nice to be near Aunt Lila, Uncle Paul and Meredith.

While New York had been exciting, it was a long way from the only home she really loved. The apartments and houses she and her parents had shared were gone. They had even put their furnishings in storage before this last assignment. Uncertain of where they would go when it was complete, they didn't want the expense of a house that would be vacant for several months.

Cooper came out of the house wearing the same casual clothes he'd worn to church, but carrying a blanked and small cooler. A dark blazer was slung over one shoulder. He tossed it all into the backseat when he opened his door and slid behind the wheel.

"I thought we'd stop at the Dairy Freeze for a burger and then head for the river. You haven't seen the new interpretive center, have you?"

"No, but Aunt Lila wrote me about it. Has it changed things a lot?"

"No. It's upstream from the swimming area. Theoretically the natural wildlife finds a haven there. There are boardwalks lining both sides of the river with signs telling you what flora and fauna is visible. We can always go swimming if you want."

"I didn't bring a suit."

"Guess that answers that. Ready?"

Leigh nodded. She'd do her best to remember all she'd read in the journal and apply everything to today's outing. Practice as well as practical, two new watchwords.

Leigh enjoyed the afternoon. But she wasn't sure Cooper did. Lunch had been quick, then they'd driven to the river. Half the families in town had the same idea. The parking lot was crowded. The boardwalk thundered with the sound of children running back and forth. The benches spaced every few hundred yards were occupied by older visitors, and even the secluded areas were filled with teenagers laughing and listing to loud music.

Cooper took Leigh's hand when they left the car. They wandered along the raised boardwalk. From time to time they had to walk single file because of others, but even then Cooper kept firm contact, shifting his hold from her hand to her shoulders.

Leigh gave up protesting and set out to enjoy the afternoon. Conversation was of necessity sporadic. But she didn't mind. She enjoyed seeing what the local town council had done to improve the river front area.

In the late afternoon Cooper took her to the swimming beach. Young children in bright life jackets played in the shallows, while older boys and girls used the two ropes suspended from overhanging branches to swing wide and drop into the deeper part of the river. Parents lounged in chairs at the river's edge.

Instantly memories of long-ago summers surfaced. Leigh and Meredith and their friends had spent many wonderful hours playing at the river. She wished she'd brought her suit to see if she could recapture some of the memories.

Another day, maybe.

"We could have gone swimming," he said as they watched the children frolic in the lazily meandering water.

"Was it this crowded when we used to swim here?"

"Sometimes. Only we were the ones in the water, so it didn't seem to matter. We should have gone somewhere else today."

Let the man do the chasing—just don't run so fast he can't catch you.

Leigh leaned a bit closer to him and her hand drifted to his shoulder. She could feel the heat beneath his shirt.

"I can't think why. I've enjoyed seeing all the changes, remembering back when I was a kid. I've had a great afternoon."

He put his arm around her and drew her closer.

"If there weren't a hundred people within eyesight, I'd take up where we left off the other afternoon."

She blinked, heat spreading throughout, washing up into her cheeks, moving swiftly all the way to her fingertips. Swallowing hard, Leigh held his gaze, slowly licking her lower lip.

Cooper groaned.

"Are you doing that deliberately to provoke me? That sexy dress is driving me crazy with the way it fits like a second skin on top and then flares out to sway and swish as you walk. Quite a change from shorts and a T-shirt. Your hair begs for my fingers to test its softness."

Even as he spoke he gently rubbed several strands.

Leigh caught her breath. The dark gleam in his eyes clearly announced his interest. Or was she reading him all wrong? How much was real, and how much wishful thinking after reading Megan's journal?

Chapter Four

The afternoon sped by and as soon as the sun began to sink, Cooper drove to the country club. Because Willow Creek was so small, there were few restaurants in town. The city of Charlotte was close enough when a couple wanted a night out. Most of the towns people belonged to the country club, so it was always well patronized.

This night was no exception. It was crowded. The Sunday buffet proved to be a popular item. Leigh and Cooper were seated at a table on the terrace, near the open area where dancing would commence later. The late afternoon sun was blocked from the terrace by the elegant brick building. Umbrellas still stood spread open over tables, their usefulness diminished as evening approached.

The tennis courts were empty, but the high night lights that had been installed a few years ago offered die-hard enthusiasts a few more hours of play after sunset. While no one was taking advantage this evening, the cooler hours after sunset made it a popular place.

"So, tell me what important plans did you finally change to come out with me today," Cooper said after they had been seated and handed menus.

"Writing a resumé," Leigh said, reaching for a roll and then offering the basket to Cooper. He stared at her, ignoring the bread.

"Writing a resumé? You almost gave up spending a day with me to write a resumé?"

Leigh looked at him innocently, almost laughing at his incredulity.

"I do have to look for another job, you know. I don't have unlimited funds. The sooner I get started, the sooner I'll find something."

"I thought you might stay for the summer or a good portion of it at least," Cooper said, taking a roll from the basket and tearing it in two.

"I'm not a child any more. I have to work," she said reasonably, wondering if he wanted her to stay for the summer. Or was he merely being polite?

"You can always write your resumé when I'm at work, spend time with me when I'm home," he said.

She laughed softly.

"You sound like a petulant little kid. I'll write it when I want. You're lucky I decided I could wait another day. Besides, nice as this is, we won't make a habit of it."

"I'm supposed to be impressed with my luck? We spent the morning with your cousin and Josiah in church, the afternoon surrounded by half the town of Willow Creek and now the other half is here for dinner."

"Aren't you glad not to have that puppy-lovestruck girl dogging your every footstep?" she asked lightly, buttering a piece of warm roll. What had she read most recently in the diary? Something about asking about his work. That should be easy. Most men liked to impress women with their accomplishments.

"Instead of dogging my footsteps, she's doing her best to

avoid me or annoy me," he grumbled, laying down the menu. "Decided what you want yet?"

Leigh looked up, her eyes bright with amusement.

"You think I'm avoiding you? Why ever would I do that?"

"You can't suggest you're the same girl who once thought she was in love with me?"

"No, of course not. Still, you took a risk asking me out for dinner, don't you think? What if I still had that crush?"

"No risk. Since you've arrived you've shown me you couldn't care less. It challenges a man, you know."

Megan had been right. Chalk one up for great-grandmothers.

"So are you now going to try to make me fall for you to meet some challenge?" she asked sassily.

And if he did? How would she feel about that? This had started as a lark, see if any of the advice from the diary actually worked. She didn't believe for an instant that Cooper would really fall for her. Or that she wanted him to. She'd grown up. Both had moved beyond the stages of their lives when she'd known him before.

And she was still uncertain what she wanted to do next. Would she stay in North Carolina, or return to New York? What she ought to do was fly to Greece and spend some weeks with her parents and look for a new job in the fall.

"No, the last thing I want is some woman thinking she's falling in love with me. Or what she imagines is love. That's nothing but a trap for unwary men." Cooper's tone took a hard edge.

"So why ask me out? Actually almost demand I go out with you?"

"For old times' sake?"

Leigh leveled him a look. "And?"

"And to get some questions answered. I haven't seen you in a long time. I wanted to discover what you're like now. Maybe we could share a few fun dates together before you move on."

"Safe and practical," she murmured, oddly disappointed.

Yet why should she feel disappointed? He proposed almost the exact terms she would have.

He nodded.

Murmuring her new watchword beneath her breath, she wryly shook her head. She didn't feel very practical sitting opposite Cooper listening to him propose they date casually. Her heart had flipped at his words, now it pounded in her chest. Her hands grew damp and she put them in her lap. The familiar tingle resonated on her skin. For one moment she almost blurted out an acceptance. Then the words of her great-grandmother echoed in her mind.

It was one thing to practice her new guidelines with Cooper, since she knew nothing would come of a relationship between them. He'd as much admitted it himself not two seconds ago. Did she still want to practice those long-ago words of wisdom?

"Thanks, I think, but I'll pass."

"Saving your time for Mr. Right?" he asked lightly.

"Just not interested. Oh, look, is that Mr. and Mrs. Gramlin?" Leigh indicated an elderly couple being shown to a table near theirs.

"Yes."

"Aunt Lila wrote me last month about their anniversary celebration."

She smiled triumphantly at Cooper.

"They have been married fifty years. See, there are marriages that last."

"So far."

Leigh laughed aloud.

"You're so cynical. That must make you one of the best lawyers around. Tell me more about your practice."

Cooper looked at her for a moment, assessment in his gaze. "What do you want to know?"

"Everything. How you like it, what gives you the greatest pleasure, what you dislike about practicing law. What cases have been unusual. Do you have a partner?"

He hesitated a moment as if not sure he knew what she expected. Then slowly he began to speak.

Leigh became instantly fascinated. Cooper had a flair for captivating her interest and holding it as he spoke of the difficulties of building a private practice, of the frustrations with all the rules and guidelines that seemed to protect the alleged criminals more than the actual victims.

He spoke of struggling alone for the first few years and then joining another firm in which he was now partner. Discussing the differences between a solo act and a team effort, his voice shimmered with enthusiasm. She took delight in his quiet confidence and pride in his successes.

The music began as they were eating dinner and by the time Leigh finished, several couples were circling the area on the terrace set aside for dancing. Time flew by as she listened to Cooper quietly discuss some of his unusual cases.

"Are you bored yet?" he asked.

"Never. It's fascinating. If I find some free time this week, I might stop in and watch you in action. You said you were in court every day, right?"

"Right. So you'd slip in like you did years ago?"

"I hope I'm a bit more adult now. I promise not to giggle."

He nodded, watching her thoughtfully.

"You've let me talk on forever. Your turn."

"Me?"

"Tell me about Leigh."

Idly she traced the rim of her glass, her eyes watching her fingertip. What could she tell him?

"I think I should defer that question until later. I'm at a crossroads now. What I defined myself as a month ago has all changed. Once I've decided what I want to do with my future, I'll probably change things again."

She looked up, catching her breath at the understanding in his dark gaze. Flustered, she glanced around, watching the couples dancing to the soft music.

"It must have been hard to lose your job. Your aunt said you loved it."

"It was hard. I don't want to talk about it now."

She fixed her gaze on a couple and wished for a moment she felt as carefree as the woman appeared. Carefree and happy.

"Looks like fun," she said, sipping the last of her iced tea.

"If you want to wait for dessert, we could dance."

"Sure."

The song was slow, the lights dimmed, the air warm and sultry. Slowly Cooper drew her close, encircling her with both arms, pulling her against the hard muscles of his chest. He linked his hands at the small of her back and started moving with the music. Leigh put her arms around his neck and rested her forehead against his cheek. The scent of his aftershave filled her, sexy and enticing. She felt young and almost starry-eyed once again. How many times as a teenager had she fantasized about dancing with Cooper, about his arms around her, her body pressed against his?

Now that those long-ago dreams had become reality, it was too late. She knew he was not the man for her. It was past time to put away childish wishes and focus on her future. Maybe Cooper had the right idea, spend some time together until she moved on. Knowing she couldn't fall for him again would safeguard her heart.

And there were still more of Megan's ingredients to test. Leigh sighed softly and tried to ignore the clamoring to snuggle closer, tried to ignore the tingling sensations that danced across her skin at Cooper's touch.

Slowly they swayed, not talking, simply enjoying the melody and the evening. The song ended and another began. Cooper didn't miss a beat. They drifted around the dance floor as if they'd been partners forever.

Leigh knew she'd never forget this night. A few magical hours out of time. She felt a bit sad. She'd have given anything to have him dance with her like this eleven years ago. That would have given her a memory to treasure.

Now, they were two strangers sharing an evening.

When the small combo took a break, Leigh excused herself to visit the rest room. While she drew a comb through her hair, she studied herself in the mirror. Her eyes were bright and sparkling, the flush on her cheeks wasn't entirely from being in the sun that afternoon. The dress was perfect. All in all, not a bad turnout. And one Cooper seemed to appreciate. Was it the novelty of having her not fawning over him that made him more interested?

Five minutes later she rejoined Cooper.

"Dessert?" he asked.

"No, just coffee. It's a beautiful night, isn't it."

"A bit warm."

"Umm."

She nodded and looked around the terrace. Waving at a friend, she noticed the area was as crowded as ever. The buffet wasn't the only attraction. It seemed the people from Willow Creek liked to dance as well.

When the music resumed, Cooper rose.

"Dance?"

"Maybe another one or two. I need to get home before too long," Leigh said.

"Right, you need to get to sleep if you're going to be writing a resumé tomorrow."

"Don't you have to go to work?"

"Yes, but I can get by on a few hours less sleep one night."

"Lucky you. Even with court tomorrow?"

"I'll manage. If you do come into Charlotte one day, I'll take you to lunch."

"Umm, I'll see," she murmured.

Once on the dance floor, Leigh gave way to impulse and snuggled closer. It was probably a once-in-a-lifetime chance. Not wanting to miss a second of it, she grly her heart pounding and hoped Cooper didn't. If nothing else, she wanted to portray a cool sophisticated woman.

Boldly, she threaded her fingers through the thick hair on the back of his head. Cooper pulled her even closer. Her skirt caught and released against his pants as they swayed and moved to the music.

"It's hot," Cooper murmured in the crush of the crowd.

The breeze from earlier had died down. Even on the patio, the night air felt sultry and warm. She smellrf the scent of jasmine. A sleepy southern night. She'd missed them living in New York.

Matching the tempo of the melody, she gave herself up to

move with the music. When Cooper's hand drifted up and down across her back, she almost melted against him.

For a second she let herself consider whether she could share more with him. If Megan's plans really worked, could she make Cooper fall in love with her?

No, his shell was too hard. His defenses firmly in place. The most she might expect was some indication that her great-grandmother's advice had some merit. Practice made perfect. Once she was assured of her direction, she'd look for a man she could love, and that would love her in return.

She wanted to share her life with someone. Make a family, set down roots and start traditions. She'd had her fling in the big city, had her shot at a career. No reason she couldn't scale back a bit to make room in her life for that family.

Cooper moved his hand across Leigh's back, surprised at the physical awareness that flared with the woman in his arms. For a moment he almost forgot this was the pest of his younger years. The unexpected desire that erupted surprised him. Normally immune to women, he wondered why he felt differently about Leigh.

She'd spent several minutes telling him she didn't plan to remain in Willow Creek forever. She really had no idea what she was going to do in the future. She'd probably return to New York and he'd not see her again for another few years.

But while she was here, he could spend some time with her. Learn what made her tick these days. Find out just why she fascinated him now.

From the first moment he'd seen her pulling into the Porters' driveway, he'd been interested. It'd been a long time and maybe he'd missed her adoration. He felt her skirt encircle his trousers, fall free as they turned and swayed. He was growing more and more intrigued with this woman. She remained a mystery, refusing to talk much about herself and instead asking him what he was doing. He wanted to know her better.

His head snapped up. It was time to call a halt to thoughts like that. His future was mapped out and it didn't include getting involved with anyone. Especially Leigh.

When the music ended, Cooper dropped his arms and guided her from the dance floor.

"Get your purse, time to go."

"So soon?"

Leigh's tone mocked. Narrowing his eyes, he looked at her. Not for an instant did he believe that innocent expression.

"What game are you playing now?" he asked.

"No game. If you want to leave, we'll leave. It is late, and you do have to work tomorrow."

She made a big production of taking another sip of her water, of looking for her purse. He glanced at her long bare legs. Did they go on forever? That sassy skirt played havoc with his senses when she walked. It swished and swayed around her, displaying, concealing. Driving him up the wall. Her skin had been velvet soft beneath his fingers. He liked touching her.

"I'll get your purse."

He reached around her and snatched it up from the floor, handing it to her. If he didn't get her out of there soon, he wouldn't be responsible for his own actions. Or reactions. And he didn't like the feeling. He'd been in charge of his own hormones for a long time now. What was going on?

Leigh remained silent on the ride home, wondering why Cooper had cut the evening short after saying he didn't need much sleep.

They'd been close tonight, she knew. Closer than ever in their lives. Talking like two friends, rather than adversaries.

Yet he'd slammed that door closed and was now the silent distant man she remembered. Had she done something to make him think she was chasing him? Thinking back, Leigh remembered nothing.

Sighing gently at the vagaries of the male species, she relaxed in her seat. At least there was no heartache attached to this. She'd bid him good-night and that would be the end.

Unless Cooper changed his attitude, she doubted she'd go out with him again. He was too unpredictable. Maybe she could practice her newfound advice on someone else. Karl had invited her out again. And Peter Jordan.

Cooper pulled into his driveway and stopped the engine.

"I'll walk you over," he said.

"No need. I can see myself home, it's just next door."

"I took you out, I'll walk you home," he said grimly.

Leigh looked at him in the dark, wishing he'd left the lights on. Even the dim glow from the dashboard would have helped gauge his expression, his mood.

"We are neighbors who went out for dinner. No big deal. I can dash across the grass and be home in a couple of seconds."

The overhead light seemed bright when he thrust open his door.

"I'll walk over with you."

It was the kind of voice no one argued with.

Leigh shrugged. A few more minutes and the evening would be finished. She had mixed emotions about the success of her venture. But Cooper wasn't an ordinary man. She shouldn't dismiss Megan's advice merely because it didn't work with him.

When he opened the passenger door, she slid out, and quickly moved toward her aunt's house. Cooper matched her step for step until they reached the porch.

Before she could open the door, he reached out to cup her face.

"A kiss good-night?" he asked softly.

"I hardly think this constitutes a date, Cooper. Just neighbors going out for dinner," she said primly.

Her heart raced. Would he really kiss her? Her mind, mouth, entire body remembered the kiss in the yard. She had no lemonade tonight, nothing to stop him if he really wanted to kiss her.

Nothing to stop him and every inch of her yearning for that kiss.

"Then a neighborly kiss," he said, lowering his head and covering her mouth with his.

Leigh knew she was in trouble the moment he touched her. Senses spinning out of control, she responded. It was unlike the kiss she'd attempted so many summers ago. Cooper was in charge, deepening the kiss, thrilling her to her toes.

She encircled his neck with her arms when his came around her. Vaguely in the back of her mind she registered his hands pressed against her back, holding her tightly against that strong, masculine body.

Then gradually sanity surfaced. Leigh pushed against his shoulders. When he released her, she spun around and entered the dark house. Closing the door, she leaned against it, trying to get her breathing under control. She'd spent the entire day telling herself not to get involved with Cooper, to try the different steps Megan had listed, but keep her heart whole. One kiss threatened her entire equilibrium.

The knock sounded impatient.

"What?" she asked, knowing it was Cooper.

She couldn't face him. She wanted to fly up to her room, climb into bed and pull the covers over her head. Maybe she should return to New York tomorrow, before she had a chance to see him. Before wild impetuous dreams took root.

"You okay?"

"Of course. Thank you for dinner. Goodbye."

Leigh leaned against the door, hearing his footsteps walk away.

Pushing away, she headed for her bedroom. She snatched up her sleep shirt and headed for the bathroom. In only moments she was ready for bed.

Now if she could only sleep. Her heart raced, her mouth still felt the press of Cooper's. And her thoughts spun round and round.

Opening her window wider for any hint of air that stirred, she stared at Cooper's house. There were lights on downstairs. Resentfully she wondered if he even gave a second thought to that devastating kiss. He turned her world topsy-turvy, and probably didn't even feel a speck of anything. Just another casual dinner to him. Probably satisfied whatever curiosity he had. No need to invite her out a second time. She'd just be another in a long line of women he took out once and never called again.

She turned away, and tried to forget.

Cooper took a sip of the whisky and waited while it burned down to his stomach. Normally not a drinking man, tonight had him wound tighter than a watch spring. It was Leigh's fault. She'd changed. And he didn't like the unsettled feelings that her change wrought. He prided himself on his ability to read witnesses, to anticipate the moves of the prosecution, and to gauge the mood of a jury.

But with Leigh, he was at a total loss.

Or was it just ego that couldn't let go of the idea she was playing some kind of game? That she still wanted him and was trying a new tactic to get his attention. For years she'd thrown herself at him. It seemed out of character for her to virtually ignore him since she'd arrived.

Yet that kiss proved she wasn't indifferent to him. He looked out the window at her place. It was dark except for her bedroom. She was still awake. Remembering their kiss?

He took another swallow. She'd tasted as sweet as hot honey. Her body had fit against his perfectly, as if they had been created for each other. Her scent had filled him, feeding the burning desire to a hot flame. He wanted her. And hadn't a clue what he was going to do about that.

He shook his head and poured another inch of amber liquid into his glass. No one person was created especially for another. And those fool enough to delude themselves that they had some special bond soon discovered the truth in an ugly fight that left both parties bitter and resentful.

His father had made sure both his sons learned that lesson well.

But there was something about Leigh that had Cooper intrigued. Trying to reconstruct the day, he realized he'd dominated the conversation. She'd asked questions about his work, about his life in Willow Creek, and given away very little about herself. He wanted to know more about what she'd been doing, how she had liked her job, the men she had dated. About her plans for the future.

Turning, he dialed the familiar number. The phone rang several times before she answered.

"Leigh, it's me, Cooper."

"Yes?"

Her wary tone made him smile.

"I didn't get you out of bed, did I?"

"Did you call just to ask dumb questions?" she replied with some asperity. "I have gone to bed, but I wasn't asleep yet. Do not call back in ten minutes to ask if I had fallen asleep."

"Don't hang up. I wanted to talk."

"We talked all day."

"I did. You're a very good listener. But I realize I learned very little about you, what you've been doing for the last few years. How you liked New York, what you did in your job, who you've been seeing."

The silence stretched out for several moments. She cleared her throat. A sign of nervousness, Cooper thought. Interesting. Why would Leigh be nervous?

"It's late, Cooper. I want to go to bed. Couldn't we have this conversation another time?"

"You name when."

He'd pin her down before hanging up.

"I don't know, I'll call you."

"Not good enough. We make a date now."

"A date?"

The wary tone in her voice startled him. Didn't she want to see him again?

"A date. Lunch Tuesday," he said.

He wasn't going to be put off by some vague promise. She could commit and he'd hold her to it.

"Tuesday's not good. I'm busy," she said quickly, almost too quickly.

"Thursday, then."

Cooper refused to get into a discussion of what constituted busy. If she said she was writing her resumé again, he'd throw the phone against the wall and storm over to talk to her in person.

"Okay, lunch Thursday."

"Come to my office and I'll give you the nickel tour."

"Fine. Good night."

She hung up.

Slowly Cooper replaced the receiver, wondering what was going on in Leigh's mind. Maybe on Thursday, he'd find out.

Thursday lunch, she thought, climbing back into bed. She should have made an excuse. That kiss showed her more than anything she was in danger of falling under his spell again if she weren't extremely careful. And she knew nothing lay in that direction but heartache.

Reaching for the old diary, Leigh flipped through to the pages she'd skimmed that morning.

Mama said I should make sure I have plenty of questions to ask about his work, and the other areas of his life. Men enjoy talking about themselves, and by doing so give us a good idea of what it would be like to be paired with them forever. If he bores me on a date, he would certainly bore me throughout a marriage. I can't imagine Frederick boring me ever. Just the sound of his voice seems to fill me with a exuberant happiness that I have never experienced before.

Leigh closed her eyes, remembering Cooper's voice. It was as smooth as Tennessee whisky and as intoxicating. His inflection carried a touch of Southern accent, but the deep richness was uniquely his own.

Megan had loved Frederick's voice, Leigh thought she loved Cooper's. He could probably read her the *Law Review* and she'd find it fascinating because he was reading it. What would it be like to hear that voice beside her in the dark? To reach out and touch him in the night and know he was near?

And if today was any indication, Cooper filled her with an exuberant happiness.

Breathless, she placed the journal on the table and flicked off the light. The darkness offered a safe haven for dreams. And Leigh knew she'd dream about Cooper.

What she needed to do was forget the impossible and concentrate on making plans for her future.

But for a few moments, she weakly gave into the daydreams of a shared life with the man next door. Imagining the kisses they'd share, the midnight hours they would fill with love and laughter.

Time enough to be practical in the morning!

Chapter Five

Leigh awoke early the next morning and for the first time in ages began to feel more like her usual self. Her energy level was approaching normal. Coming to North Carolina had been the best thing for what ailed her, she thought whimsically as she lay in bed and listened to the birds chirping and trilling. It'd undoubtedly be hot again today, but she didn't care. Her dresses were cool and comfortable. And she'd done all the yard work she needed to do for a few days.

Donning one of the new sundresses, Leigh lightly applied makeup and brushed her hair. She made her bed, darting a quick glance at the house next door. All was silent.

Cooper's car was gone. He had to work today and had obviously already left for Charlotte.

The memory of his kiss jumped into her mind and Leigh took a deep breath, trying to calm her instantly-ragged nerves. It was too late for regrets and might-have-beens. She knew that. This was simply an interlude in her life. Once she decided what to do next, she could throw all her energies into that and forget the sexy neighbor who had one time filled her dreams.

Today, however, she had nothing pressing and planned to take one step at a time.

Fixing a light breakfast, she read the local paper, jotted notes of things she wanted to be sure to include in her resumé, and savored the delicious hazelnut coffee her aunt loved so much. If she'd still been in New York, by this hour she'd have already attended two meetings, placed a dozen phone calls and be scrambling to get everything accomplished in a hectic day.

For a moment she remembered. It had been exhilarating and exciting. But gone now. There was no urgency to her day.

Leigh took her second cup of coffee, and the old journal, and went to sit on one of the wicker rockers on the front porch. Across the street the Bandeleys were leaving together. She waved. They'd lived there since long before she started making her annual summer visits. Friends of her aunt and uncle's, they'd had no children.

Idly Leigh wondered if she was destined to remain single. Or would she one day find a man to whom she'd be able to apply great-grandma Megan's strategy. Would they be blessed with children? The lack hadn't been detrimental to the Bandeley's marriage. They still appeared very much in love.

Another example she could hold up for Cooper. She smiled wickedly. He didn't seem to like her models of marital bliss.

In fact, when she thought about it, his parents were the only ones in the neighborhood who had split. In this case, his family was the anomaly, not the rule.

Had he ever thought of that, she wondered.

Sipping the delicious coffee, she turned to Megan's journal.

Aunt Dottie came to tea today. She asked me how I was faring and I told her about Frederick. She laughed and exchanged glances with Mama, then told me to always remember to keep a man guessing. To keep a mystical aura that will have him wondering what I'm thinking. Do the unexpected, she told me. Don't let a man become complacent. Keep him guessing. Try something outrageous and see how he takes it. Life is long: if your husband can't be open to new ideas, you'll be unhappy.

Mama laughed and nodded. Sage advice, she said. I use it with your father.

Turning eighteen is a wondrous time, at last the other women consider me an adult and are sharing their worldly wisdom. Tonight, I'll try that with Frederick. He is coming to escort me to the church social. What can I do that he would find unexpected?

A few minutes later Leigh gazed across the lawn, a smile on her face. Megan was a gem. She wished she could have known her. For an idle moment she wondered what she could do that Cooper would find unexpected.

Maybe ignoring him was enough. That was certainly unexpected given her past infatuation. Though she thought Megan would consider that remained as a hard-to-get step. Was there truly any correlation between her behavior and the fact Cooper seemed more interested this visit than ever before? Or was it just coincidence?

Time would prove it, one way or the other. And time was something she had in abundance.

The few days she'd spent in Willow Creek had already begun to heal. She didn't miss her job as much as she thought she would. She did miss some of her fellow workers, but most of them had been let go as well and were either already working for another firm or still searching for a new position.

Which was what she should be doing. First, however, she had to decide where to look. New York was exciting, energizing, dynamic. But a bit lonely, even with good friends.

Here she had family and longtime friends. Charlotte was a fast-growing metropolitan area with jobs that would offer the same kind of challenge as the one she'd loved so much. And if she were closer to home, wouldn't that be an added fillip? Yes.

Her decision made, Leigh spent the rest of the morning working on her resumé. In the afternoon she went to the country club to swim and lie in the sun. Time enough to be ambitious when she was fully recovered from burnout. This was a well-earned vacation and she planned to take full advantage of every moment.

Whiling away the afternoon let her spin ways she could appear totally unexpected to Cooper Bryant. What would surprise that jaded cynic? Nothing obvious or trite. She needed to come up with something totally different from his usual routine and hers.

Being mysterious wouldn't work. He knew too much about her. Her aunt, she was sure, kept him apprised of major events. Her parents had visited a couple of years ago and mentioned they'd talked to Cooper.

No, mysterious wouldn't work. But doing the unexpected might. But what?

Just before she slipped into a light nap, the perfect escapade occurred to her. Smiling, she knew it'd surprise him as nothing had in ages.

If she could pull it off.

Leigh fixed a light meal for supper, eating it before the television. She'd spent a little too much time in the sun and her glowing skin was tender to the touch. By tomorrow her skin would begin to tan, but tonight she felt like a lobster.

Considering an early evening, she surfed through the different channels on the TV. Nothing caught her attention or held her interest. Maybe she should read more of Megan's journal. It was so much fun. She hated to read straight through because then she'd be finished. Even though her curiosity hummed, she liked savoring each entry. Maybe one more example today wouldn't hurt.

Washing her dishes, she retrieved the journal and sat in one of the wicker rockers on the front porch.

The evening breeze cooled the air, carrying with it the soft fragrance of roses and star jasmine. The scents were a tangible reminder she was truly home. Until she smelled it, she hadn't realized how much she'd missed the sweet fragrances in New York.

Cooper's car wasn't in his driveway. Was he working late? Or did he have a hot date tonight? Leigh frowned, not liking the idea. Not that she expected him to date her, but for some reason he seemed a loner. Yet she knew he hadn't been sitting around for years while she moved on in life. Even though Celia had turned him off relationships, he was a virile, healthy male, not likely to remain at home alone.

Thinking about Cooper dating sophisticated women made Leigh restless. She fixed a glass of iced tea and sipped it. Watching his driveway wasn't the way she wanted to spend her evening, she thought in disgust when she realized what she was doing. Going inside, she firmly shut the door. She had better things to do than watch for her next-door neighbor. What he did with his evenings didn't affect her.

Yet she couldn't help but notice the time when she heard his car two hours later. It was after nine. Too early to end a date. Maybe he'd worked late after all. Her restlessness faded.

Cooper pulled into his driveway and stopped, glad to be home. He was bone weary. Court cases always took a lot of energy and today's session hadn't gone well. Even after working in this profession for years, it amazed him that clients would lie. Why couldn't they understand their best interests were always served when they told their attorney the truth in everything? He hated to be blindsided in court as he had been today.

As a result, instead of leaving the office at a reasonable hour, he'd had to call in the investigating team. Together they'd worked to find a solution to the unexpected turn of events. Normally he didn't mind working late. But tonight he'd wanted to get home earlier.

He climbed out of the car and glanced at the house next door. The downstairs lights were on. Leigh was still up. For a split second he hesitated. What he'd really like to do was walk over there and see her. Find out what she'd done that day, and maybe share a bit of his own frustrations.

Heading for his front door, he shook off the urge. Give that woman an inch and she'd take a mile. He dare not show any interest lest she take it for more than he intended and resume her schoolgirl crush.

Or would she?

The last few days had been a totally new experience with Leigh. All evidence indicated she was no longer interested in any kind of relationship.

Perversely, he wished she wanted to spend time with him. Opening the door, he noticed how empty the house seemed, how quiet. Maybe he'd see if she'd like to come keep him company while he ate. It'd be worth having someone around to take his mind off the day's events. A man could spend too much time alone.

He reached for the phone.

When she answered, Cooper was startled at the jolt of awareness that crashed through him. Her voice was feminine and sweet, without the strong Southern drawl so many women he knew had. She had very little accent from any location—an obvious result of her moving so often as a child. Had she liked moving all the time? Funny, he'd never asked her that.

"Leigh, it's Cooper."

"What's up?"

"What are you doing?"

"Getting ready for bed, why?"

Instantly the image of her in a frilly sexy gown flashed before his eyes. Her arms would be bare, the neckline scooped to show her creamy shoulders and the top swells of her breasts. It would drift around her legs like her dress had the other night, soft and feminine and utterly alluring.

Alluring? Leigh? He was losing it.

"Isn't it a bit early?"

He loosened his tie, shrugged off his suit jacket and tossed on the back of the sofa.

"I'm on vacation, I can do what I want, when I want."

"Still, it's early. Come over."

The silence lasted longer than he expected.

"Come over?"

"I just got home and could use some company."

"Take it from an expert, Cooper, working all hours doesn't pay off. I used to do that, but it's more important to have outside activities. Something to fall back on if something happens."

He smiled. Was she lecturing him?

"What's going to happen?"

"I don't know, you could lose your job."

"I'm a partner in the firm, I won't lose my job. There is always a need for lawyers."

"I guess."

He leaned against the wall, staring through the window toward her house. Where was she? Was she already dressed for bed?

"What did you do today?" he asked.

If she wasn't coming over, he'd talk on the phone. He wasn't ready to hang up and face the rest of the evening alone.

"Did you call me up to interrogate me about my day?"

"I called you to invite you over. You're the one getting ready for bed. Wearing that slinky nightie?"

Her voice dropped to a deep, sultry drawl, "Cooper, honey, I can't believe you'd ask me what I'm wearing. Why, what if I told you I had nothing on at all? It's been hot all day and I'm so uncomfortable, I just couldn't bear the thought of covering myself with hot clothes. I like the feel of the cool air against my bare skin. I like the freedom of movement without the restrictions of cloth."

Stunned, he could envision that with no trouble. Except for the trouble he had breathing. The trouble he had even thinking.

Her soft laughter floated across the phone wire.

"Gotcha," she said softly and hung up.

Torn between frustration and amusement, Cooper hung up. Leigh surprised him. He'd never expected anything like that from her. He had to admit he'd thought she'd jump at the chance to come over. Though he should have known better.

Nothing she'd done since she'd returned had been in character as he remembered. It wasn't a game. She'd changed since the last time he'd seen her.

Now he was curious about what other aspects would catch him unaware? He had half a mind to go over there and demand she open the door, just to verify she was teasing—that she actually had clothes on.

He punched in the number again.

"Hello?"

"Leigh, you could get in a lot of trouble leading people on."

She laughed. The sound warmed him to his toes. What was there about her that caught his attention this visit?

"Didn't expect that, huh?"

"Not at all. Do you lie in bed at night and think up things like that?"

"Almost. Today I thought it up by the pool."

"Any more tricks up your sleeve?"

"Why, Cooper, didn't you hear me? I'm not wearing sleeves, I'm—"

"You're playing with fire. If you keep that up I'll have to come over to check to see exactly what you are wearing. Or you can come over here."

"Thank you for the invitation, but I really am getting ready to go to bed soon. Why are you so late coming home?"

"Had some work to catch up on tonight and no, it couldn't wait. I'm due in court tomorrow at nine and had to get all the facts straight before then. Did you go to bed this early in New York?"

"Of course not. Maybe if I had I wouldn't be so tired now."

"Tell me something about living in the Big Apple."

"Why?"

"You cross-examined me to the *n*th degree at dinner last night, don't you think turnabout is fair play?"

"I'd hardly call it cross-examining you. I merely asked a couple of questions."

"And now I'm asking some. Tell me about New York."

She hesitated at first, but soon began to offer brief sketches of her apartment, her job and a few friends. She was strangely quiet on the topic of boyfriends. And for some reason, Cooper didn't want to ask. Another time she could regale him with her romantic conquests.

Tonight, he liked listening to her, trying to understand the hectic and exciting lifestyle she'd enjoyed for the last few years. A world of difference from Willow Creek. But not too different from Charlotte's pace.

When he recognized some of the product brands she'd worked with at the marketing firm, he was startled. He hadn't realized her job had been so important, so national in scope. Obviously he needed to reassess his thinking.

"So there you have it in a nutshell. I saw the Bandeleys today."

He'd been coasting, listening to her talk, and trying to remember all the nuances of her expression as he imagined her face while she entertained him on the phone.

"What do they have to do with New York?"

"Nothing, I'm changing the subject. They'e a happy couple, wouldn't you say?"

"As far as I know."

"Umm. Another happily married couple. And they're not young. They seemed old when I first came to visit as a little kid."

"The point to this being?"

"Only mentioning another couple who've had a long happy marriage. You should consider that, counselor. Good night, Cooper. I'm really going to bed now."

He bid her good-night and hung up, surprised to see it was almost eleven. Debating whether to eat anything or just go to bed himself, he wondered why she'd brought up the neighbors.

Did she still think of him in a romantic manner? She'd done nothing to suggest that this visit. No throwing herself at him, no flirting. Unless her kisses could count. Or rather her responses to his kisses. Yet she kept bringing up happily married couples. What was her game? The old defenses rose.

If she thought to convince him to change his mind, to give marriage a try, and with her, she didn't know him at all. He'd made up his mind years ago and nothing had happened in the intervening years to change it. Nothing would.

Leigh turned off the lights and opened her window wide. The breeze still blew from the west, cooling her room, feeling soft and balmy against her skin. She grinned, remembering her daring conversation with Cooper.

Had that caught him by surprise?

She wished she could have seen his face.

"Is that what you meant, Megan?" she asked softly into the night.

One incident, however, wouldn't be enough. She needed to keep him off guard.

And her idea from that afternoon still seemed strong. She'd try to surprise the man again. And maybe again.

She was having fun, she realized. Feeling young and carefree, she could do whatever she wanted, as long as she knew it was for fun. There was no permanent future with Cooper. Bbut to tease him and practice her grandmother's tactics was proving to be quite a lark. Who knew how far she could take this? She couldn't wait to find out.

Once in bed, she reached for the journal. What had Great-grandma Megan come up with to keep Frederick on his toes?

Leigh planned her unexpected event with the precision of a general going into a major battle. Working for years as a project supervisor and then a manager stood her in good stead. While she tried to anticipate all the different contingencies, she didn't spend endless hours worrying about it. What happened happened.

She hoped she could pull it off. It would be fun and show

Cooper Bryant not to take her or any woman for granted in the future.

But if it didn't work, she'd shrug and move on.

Thursday morning she dressed in another of her new dresses. This one was of soft yellow, with small daisies scattered throughout the material. The bodice clung to her figure, the thin straps giving the illusion of holding up the dress. Her slight case of sunburn had mellowed into a golden tan. Brushing her sun-streaked hair until it gleamed, she was pleased that the new cut required little care. Curls danced against her head as she hurried downstairs. The long scarf she'd draped around her neck trailed behind her.

Operation Unexpected was about to begin.

She hadn't spoken with Cooper since their phone conversation the other evening.

Last night she had taken the phone off the hook. Playing hard-to-get required a lot of forward planning. Megan hadn't had it that bad. Of course people moved more slowly in those days. Leigh couldn't help but wonder if Cooper tried calling last night. And if so, what had he thought when the line was continually busy?

She drove to Charlotte and found a parking place close to Cooper's office building. A sign, she thought, pleased with the proximity. Gathering her purse, Leigh checked one last time that everything was in place. Taking a deep breath, she headed inside the high-rise building.

Studying the other women as she waited in the busy lobby for the elevator, she was pleased to note none looked as carefree and adventuresome as she felt. Their somber suits or elegant business attire seemed a world away from what she planned for today.

Yet just a few short weeks ago she'd have matched their attire and scoffed at anyone dressed as casually as she was. Excitement bubbled up inside. She couldn't wait to see Cooper's reaction.

The law firm occupied the entire eighth floor. The elevator opened directly into the reception area.

The young receptionist smiled a friendly greeting. Leigh told her she was to meet Cooper and the woman had obviously been briefed because she nodded immediately.

"He's expecting you, but he's been held up in court. They should be recessing soon."

"Not a problem. Actually, I came early for a reason. I need your help."

Leaning closer, glancing around to make sure no one was within hearing distance, she shared her plans with the young woman.

Delighted to hear the laughter that greeted her, Leigh nodded, "So I can count on your help?"

"Absolutely! I wouldn't miss this for anything. Though I have to warn you, he'll likely explode. Most of the partners have an inflated sense of their own worth."

Leigh waved a hand dismissingly.

"I can handle Cooper Bryant. We've known each other since we were kids."

Pointing out his office, the receptionist smiled broadly.

"Good luck. I might just try something like this myself—if it works."

Leigh headed for Cooper's office, hoping it would work. It was as unexpected as she could come up with on short notice. Wondering what she could devise given enough time, Leigh mentally rehearsed every step in her plan.

Keeping an eye on the elevator from the slightly ajar door, she waited impatiently. Now that she was here, she waited impatiently for Cooper to show up. Did this delay in court mean his lunch time would be shortened? Should she change her plans? Delay them for another day?

The elevator door slid open and Cooper and two others stepped out. He spoke to them and then turned to head for his office, barely acknowledging the receptionist's greeting. Leigh gave thanks he didn't seem to notice the brimming amusement in the woman's eyes.

Moving behind the door, Leigh waited, slowly pulling away her scarf.

Cooper entered.

Leigh threw the scarf around his eyes, and fastened it snugly.

"What the hell?"

His hands immediately yanked on the scarf.

"Hold it, mister," she said trying to disguise her voice.

Afraid the laughter that threatened would give it all away, she took a deep breath.

"This is an official kidnapping."

He hesitated, then dropped his hands and turned around, making no further attempt to remove the covering from his face.

"Official kidnapping?"

"Uh-huh. Don't make me get rough."

Leigh tried to keep her voice low, wondering if Cooper was fooled for a single second. He was so tall, and looked good enough to eat in his lightweight suit and the pristine white shirt with the silver-and-red tie.

Slowly one side of his mouth raised in a half smile.

"Rough? I'm fascinated."

"Good."

She reached around him to tighten the scarf so it wouldn't slip. When she pressed against him, his arms came around and before she could move he held her pinned tightly against his chest.

"This is an interesting development," he murmured softly.

"Unexpected would you say?" she asked, conscious of his strength, the long hard body held against hers.

"I've never been kidnapped before, officially or unofficially," he murmured.

"There's always a first time," she replied, knowing she should push away but was totally captivated by the sensations that filled her, that set every nerve ending tingling.

Then to Leigh's surprise, he kissed her.

"Is that the ransom?" he asked a moment later.

She could scarcely think, much less make sense of his statement.

"What?"

"Is my release dependent upon a kiss?"

"No. What time do you have to be back in court?"

"At two."

She pushed against him and stepped back as soon as he released her. Slapping his hands when he raised them to remove the scarf, she took one in hers, startled when he laced his fingers through hers.

"Behave and you'll be back in plenty of time," she said, remembering at the last moment to disguise her voice.

"And if not?"

Amusement danced in his tone.

"Just come quietly."

She opened the door and led him out. The receptionist

covered her mouth to muffle her laughter as her eyes watched Leigh lead Cooper to the elevator. Leigh looked around. There weren't many people around, but those that were stopped and watched them, wide smiles on their faces.

Fortunately there were only two businessmen in the elevator when they got on. Both looked stunned at the tall man wearing a suit blindfolded by a yellow scarf. One studied Leigh, looking almost wistful. But no one said a word when she raised her finger to her lips. Leigh gripped Cooper's hand tightly. She hoped he wouldn't be mad. If he were, he could have removed the scarf by now. Maybe he'd go along with this.

"Come on," she urged when the reached the ground floor.

Trying to avoid all the stares and laughter, Leigh led her captive through the bustling crowd in the lobby and out to the sidewalk. Thank goodness she'd been able to park close by.

The few moments it took to get Cooper into the car seemed endless. Flushed with embarrassment and triumph, she ran to the driver's side. In seconds they were away.

"Is it in order for me to inquire where we are going?" he asked relaxing in the seat.

"You'll see."

"Then at some point I do get to remove the scarf?"

"I'll do that."

"You forgot to disguise your voice," he commented dryly.

"Did you know it was me?"

"From the first."

Well, at least he wasn't kissing just anyone. If he'd known it was her, he'd meant to kiss her. Leigh licked her lips, tasting Cooper again. Excitement still bubbled.

"How?"

"Next time, don't wear honeysuckle perfume. It's unique to you."

Leigh ignored him as she found her way to the park she had in mind. It was large, with a children's play area at one end and several acres of grassy meadow. Parking, she lifted the picnic basket and blanket from the back and went to let Cooper out. When he stood, she wrapped his hand around the handle.

"You can carry this."

Taking his free hand, she led the way to a stretch of level grass.

"Okay, you can take off the scarf," she said.

"I thought you'd do that," he replied.

Eyeing him uncertainly, she reached up to loosen the material. He didn't move and when the scarf came away, he blinked once and gazed down at her.

"I thought we could have a picnic," she said, gesturing around the park, watching him warily, trying to gauge how he felt by the gleam in his eye.

"A simple invitation would have been too much, I suppose."

She shrugged, amusement dancing now that she knew he wasn't angry.

"Isn't this more exciting?"

Cooper stared at her for a long moment, then slowly nodded.

"I've never been kidnapped before. Do you make a habit of it?"

Relieved, Leigh began to shake out the blanket.

"No, my first venture. But if it turns out well, I might try again."

Cooper placed the basket on the edge of the blanket and took off his suit jacket. Unfastening his cuffs, he rolled the sleeves back before sitting.

Leigh sank to her knees, her dress billowing around her. Reaching for the basket, she quickly unpacked.

Her aunt loved romantic things and the picnic basket was no exception. China plates, silver utensils and delicate wineglasses soon were in place. She removed the food containers and opened them all. Glancing around to make sure everything was as she wanted, she looked at Cooper.

"This is your idea of a picnic?" he asked, looking at the elegant setting.

Leigh nodded, hoping he'd like it.

"You're full of surprises, Leigh Gaffney."

"And is that good?"

"Today, it's very good," he said.

Chapter Six

Cooper studied her smiling face. For a moment he went with the moment. No one had ever kidnapped him. He was startled she'd even think of doing such a thing.

Yet, wasn't that part of Leigh's past—doing outrageous things. Like the time she tried to get him to kiss her. She'd declared her love for him and he'd turned away.

Had that been the end of her infatuation? Was that the reason she kept her distance this visit until today? He'd been angry at the world at that time, still hurting over Celia. He'd wanted to ruthlessly end Leigh's devotion. Had he hurt her that day?

For a moment a pang of regret hit. He hadn't been kind to the young girl who'd followed him so faithfully.

He pushed thoughts of the past away. Today was a fresh day. They had a couple of hours to share and he wouldn't let the past intrude.

And this unexpected picnic was a great idea. Suddenly he had a thought.

"How many people saw us come out of the building?" he asked, wondering why he hadn't objected.

Was it the novelty? Or had he just been unable to upset her plan?

She grinned and heaped fresh potato salad on his plate. Using tongs, she grasped a piece of fried chicken and daintily set it on the china.

"Lots. Several had their phone out taking pictures. Will your reputation forever be tarnished?"

He could feel her high spirits as he shook his head.

"I'm in hopes the blindfold covered my face so no one knew."

"Everyone at your work knew," she said gleefully. "And if it works out, your receptionist is going to try it with her boyfriend."

Suddenly she looked stricken.

Was it the word boyfriend? Cooper wondered if Leigh still harbored feelings for him. None had been evident since she'd returned. But maybe she was better at hiding how she felt these days.

"The rolls may still be warm," she said quickly. "I baked them just before I left and wrapped them well."

She offered the covered basket.

"When was the last time you went on a picnic?" she asked.

Cooper paused in eating to try to remember.

"It's been a long time. And I've never been on one as elaborate as this."

His father wasn't a man to indulge in tomfooleries such as a picnic. It was all he could do to get through the days after his wife left. He hadn't spent time in doing many things with his boys.

"Meredith and I love picnics. We used to go on them all the time as kids. Remember that section in the stretch of woods just beyond the river? We found a clearing there when we were twelve. It was our favorite spot to eat and then lie on our backs and watch clouds drift by. It was partially shaded by the trees, so was cool even in the heat of summer. Wine? I know you have to work this afternoon, but one small glass can't hurt, right?"

"Are you coming to court today?"

"Yes. I want to see Perry Mason in action."

Her smile made him catch his breath. Her eyes sparkled and Cooper almost forgot about eating. He'd like to lean closer and—

Slamming down on the thought, he nodded, sipped the wine and watched her as she ate her own lunch. What was going on in her mine, he wondered cynically. She'd done her best to ignore him ever since she'd arrived. Ignore him or drive him crazy. Now this. A romantic picnic for two. Did it mean anything or was she just filling her days until she found a new job?

"Any luck in the job hunting?" he asked.

"I've got a dynamite resumé ready to go. But I'm not in a huge hurry to find something. Maybe in a week or two. In the meantime, I want to enjoy myself."

She took a sip of wine and glanced around the park.

"I never did this in New York," she said thoughtfully. "I think I'm going to make a major lifestyle change and opt for a slower pace of life. Why shouldn't I enjoy things as I go along?"

"I thought you liked your life in New York."

"I did, it was great. But now that things have changed, I have to consider whether I want to go back to something like that. I really threw myself into my job. Then in a single day it was gone."

Cooper nodded, knowing he'd feel totally adrift if he couldn't practice law. It was logical and orderly, yet challenging affording him the opportunity to make a difference in people's lives. Finding new ways to influence decisions was exhilarating.

Leigh talked about nonessentials as they ate. When finished, she packed up the picnic basket and looked expectantly at him.

"Did you enjoy this?" she asked almost diffidently.

Cooper nodded, surprised to realize how much he had enjoyed their novel adventure. Maybe he was getting too set in routine.

And maybe he was getting too close to Leigh when he realized how good he felt to see her smile.

"Time to head back," he said abruptly, standing and rolling down his sleeves.

He had work to do and no time to spend getting close to this woman, or any woman.

She rose and began to fold the blanket, her manner subdued. He hadn't meant to ruin the mood, just needed to get back on track. It had been a brief, fun interlude, now it was time to go back to reality.

"I appreciate your making lunch," he said. He frowned, sounding too formal and polite. Couldn't he at least put enough enthusiasm in his voice to bring that sparkle back in her eyes?

"Good, I didn't want you to be angry."

Leigh turned to head for the car. Cooper shrugged into his suit jacket and followed. Her skirt swayed as she walked, brushing against her long legs, mesmerizing in its tempo. She looked pretty, he realized. Prettier than he remembered. And sexier. Her legs were long and tanned. Her feet arched daintily in her sandals. And her hair was so shiny and glossy, it appeared to capture the sunlight.

Rubbing his fingers across his eyes, Cooper picked up his pace. He wasn't one to give in to foolish, romantic descriptions. Her hair was clean. Her legs lightly tanned. He'd seen a hundred women look as good.

Only for a moment, he couldn't remember a single other one.

He joined her before she reached the car and took the picnic basket.

"I have to stop by the office before returning to court. Let me have the keys, I'll drive."

Leigh hand the keys over, feeling generally satisfied. The

picnic had gone well. And she almost hugged herself with the delight in Cooper's comment that she proved to be unexpected. She wished Great-grandma Megan was still alive, she'd have loved to share the event with her.

Maybe she'd call Meredith tonight to tell her about the picnic. Or stop by and see her. Since her cousin hadn't read all the journal, Leigh could entertain her with some of Megan's stories.

What further things could she do to prove unexpected, she wondered as they entered the courtroom a short time later. Cooper indicated several rows of chairs where she could have a seat, then moved down the center aisle to the defendant's table. Ignoring the rows he'd indicated, she moved across the aisle so she had a better view of the man while he worked.

He was impressive. Calm and logical in his presentations, his questions to witnesses were hard-hitting and insightful. A curious blend of cynicism and compassion kept every eye on him while he was examining the witnesses.

Leigh enjoyed the afternoon, fascinated to see this side of Cooper. She remembered the day she and Meredith had come to watch him. She'd been too young then to fully appreciate the talent of the man. And he'd just been a beginner. Today she basked in his performance. If she ever needed an attorney, she'd pick Cooper in a heartbeat.

As the afternoon drew to a close, Leigh reluctantly slipped from the courtroom. Something else unexpected, she hoped, as she wandered through the cool hallways down to the first level of the old courthouse.

She knew Cooper expected her to be there when he finished. And a few years ago she would have been. But she'd grown beyond foolish infatuations in the intervening years. Even if she still had that crush on the man, she wouldn't be so blatant in her attempts to capture his interest.

Their relationship was solely that of neighbors, despite her fun at trying out the suggestions of her great-grandmother.

Leigh swung by Meredith's apartment. Finding her cousin at a loose end, they ordered in pizza and rented a movie. While they ate, Leigh shared her lunch escapade, embellishing it where she could to make it sound even more fantastic.

Meredith laughed when Leigh got to the part about blindfolding Cooper with a yellow chiffon scarf.

"I can't believe you'd even try such a thing! And I can't believe that he let you do it."

Leigh grinned in remembrance.

"It was surprising. Maybe he needs some fun in his life. For a moment I thought he'd snatch it off, but then he left it."

And kissed her silly, but she didn't need to tell her cousin everything. Some things were just too private, too special to be shared.

"And you got that idea from Megan's journal?" Meredith asked when Leigh finished her tale.

"No, just the idea of doing the unexpected. But I figured the last thing a staid respectable attorney did was get kidnapped."

Chuckling, Meredith tilted her head.

"So is he falling for you?"

Leigh looked at her cousin warily.

"No way. I don't want him to. Plus, he's made his position clear on numerous towns about not getting involved in a relationship."

The niggling voice that whispered *liar* was ignored. She'd learned her lesson. No more tilting against windmills.

"Then why are you doing this?"

"For fun, mostly. I really worked hard these last years. And I almost feel betrayed, Where's my reward for all that hard work? I was fired."

"Let go, downsized, it's different from being fired," Meredith said.

"It doesn't feel any different. I still don't have a job. I'll be thirty soon. Time to live a bit, don't you think? Anyway this is turning out to be fun. And if it looks like it's working, I can try it out on some man I might want to develop a permanent relationship with."

"What if Cooper falls for you?"

"Get real, Meredith. He's sworn off women for life. You told me how hard it is to get him to even go out with someone. Do you really think he's going to fall for me? Especially when he's done his best to push me away all our lives?"

"Doesn't seem to be pushing you away now."

Memories of recent kisses flashed into Leigh's mind. They meant nothing. Nothing beyond a momentary impulse.

"Leopards don't change their spots," Leigh murmured.

Hadn't she just read that before falling to sleep last night? She'd have to reread that passage in Megan's diary again. In fact, when Meredith finished the journal after her, she might reread it, to make sure she hadn't missed anything.

"So what are you going to do next?" Meredith asked.

"About Cooper? Nothing. You want to come to dinner on Saturday? I'll cook jambalaya. You always like that."

"I love that. I'm so glad your parents moved all around so you have a wide selection of cooking treats. Can I invite Josiah?"

Leigh shrugged.

"If you want."

"Then you'll have to invite someone so we'll be even," Meredith said slyly.

"I'll ask Karl."

Meredith wrinkled her nose.

"No. Invite Cooper. He and Josiah are good friends."

"I guess."

For some reason she was reluctant to include Cooper in her dinner plans. Was she taking the hard-to-get stance too seriously?

Suddenly she didn't want him to think for an instant she was chasing him. She'd been so embarrassed as a teenager when he'd rounded on her and blasted her for her clinging ways. There was no future in a relationship with her sexy next-door neighbor. Maybe she should repeat that litany a hundred times a day until she completely believed it.

When Leigh slowed for the turn into her driveway later that night, she saw Cooper's car parked in his. Lights shone from his house, but she didn't pause. Driving to the back, she stopped and quietly entered her aunt's home.

She thought dinner with Meredith would be the thing to do, but now she had mixed emotions. Maybe she should have stayed after court and seen what Cooper might have suggested. Dinner in Charlotte? Or would he have had more work to do and merely thanked her again for lunch?

She got ready for bed, donning her comfortable sleep T-shirt. Maybe tomorrow she'd go shopping for some really sexy nightgown. Though what would be the point, except to feel luxuriously daring when she went to bed.

She reached for the journal, but it wasn't on the night stand. Hurriedly she went downstairs and hunted for it. Where had she left it? There, in the kitchen on the table. Was she getting absent-minded? No, she remembered now. She'd brought it down to read at breakfast and been sidetracked by the local paper.

Snuggled beneath the sheet, she turned to the page she'd

skimmed before falling asleep last night.

A leopard won't change his spots. By the time a man is grown, he's set in his ways. And all the blandishments a woman tries won't change a thing. Aunt Dottie told me that this afternoon after she had taken a short nap. We were sitting in the backyard snapping beans. I love Dottie, she's a wealth of information which she freely gives. Much more so than Mama. Study the man and understand him, she said. He won't change. The woman who thinks she can change a man is forever doomed to failure. So I must make sure I can live with the man the way he is.

Frederick is a bit somber sometimes. I think he needs someone in his life to make him laugh more. But I like him. He's kind to others, listens to me, even when I try to get him to talk about himself, and is generous in his compliments. He said he found the dress I wore to the church social elegant and refined. I wouldn't want to change him. Just make him like me a little. Is he the man for me? To marry and spend the rest of my life with? I feel I could do that. Would I be enough for him?

Leigh closed the book. Cooper certainly wouldn't change at this late date. The man was thirty-four years old. Firmly established in his career and his life. He had everything just the way he wanted, Leigh thought. No need for changes. When he wanted companionship, he asked a woman out. When he wanted solitude, he went home alone.

He'd spoken the truth all those years ago. There was no future together. She stopped to admit that deep down inside she'd hoped following Megan's old-fashioned advice would cause a change of heart in the man.

She secretly still yearned for more from him. For a spark of affection or closeness that would bind them together.

Foolish thoughts, Leigh decided, switching off the light. She had no more chance of that happening than of flying to the moon. Time to end the fun and move to more serious ventures.

he could begin with sending out her resumé, and start to date other men. Maybe she would invite Karl to dinner Saturday instead of Cooper. Josiah could handle it, and she wasn't sure she wanted to spend more time with a man who really didn't want to be with her.

Not that it'd be easy. Years ago she'd been in love with Cooper. He set a standard that proved hard to match. Yet somewhere in the world there had to be a man for her. Her perfect soul mate. She just had to find him.

Cooper watched as the light in Leigh's room was extinguished. He sat in a chair in the yard, a beer forgotten in his hand. She'd come home an hour ago. Never even glanced in his direction. He almost called to her, but hesitated too long. She'd slipped inside.

Staring at the dark house, he wondered where she'd gone after disappearing from the courtroom. He didn't even know when she'd left. One moment he'd seen her from the corner of his eye, the next time he noticed she was no longer there.

Had she grown bored? Litigation was a time-consuming, sometimes tedious task. He knew everyone didn't find the same fascination with the subject as he did. But he'd wanted to hear her views of the afternoon. See how it compared to her visit with Meredith years before.

He admitted he wanted to see that rapt attention she'd shown Sunday night when he'd talked about his job. She'd acted as if it were the most fascinating topic under the sun. Grimacing briefly, Cooper wondered how she did that. Had she added acting to her skills? Or had she genuinely been interested?

Expecting her to fawn over him at the close of court, he'd been surprised to find her gone. Another unexpected view of the woman he was beginning to think he didn't know at all.

Lunch had been unexpected. Her conversation lately was different. Either she flirted like she would with anyone or she hung on his every word. Heady feeling for a man who spent most of his evenings alone.

His life suited him. He refused to open himself up to the fallacy of love.

But sometimes he got lonely. Did Leigh ever get lonely?

He rose and headed for her house. She'd proved she had unexpected impulses today with that picnic. He'd taken a bit of razzing when he returned to the office. But he wasn't mad. It'd been surprisingly fun. Maybe frivolity was something he'd been missing for a while.

Knocking on the back door, he waited impatiently. She couldn't be asleep, she'd just turned off the light a few moments ago. Knocking again, he wondered if he was going to have to break into the house to see her.

The back porch light came on and Leigh opened the door a crack and peeked out.

"Good heavens. Cooper. What's wrong?"

She opened the door and looked at him, then beyond to the dark yard.

Cooper stared at her. Unless she'd changed in an instant, she didn't wear sexy nightgowns to bed. Yet the soft cotton T-shirt that draped her suddenly seemed as exotic as any lace and satin creation ever could. Her breasts were firm and high, and clearly delineated beneath the shirt. Its hem reached her thighs, baring her long legs. Cooper's gaze traveled down the length of her and then slowly rose until he stared into her wide puzzled eyes.

"Cooper?"

"Sometimes others can do the unexpected," he murmured.

Reaching out, he caught her wrist and gently pulled until she stepped forward.

"Come with me."

He had no idea where he was going, just that he wanted to be with this provocative woman. He wanted to hear how she liked his performance in court. Tell her what he thought would happen when the case went to the jury. Spend some of the magic of the midnight hour with her.

She resisted, but he kept walking until she half skipped to catch up.

"Wait a minute. I'm not even dressed. We can't go anywhere."

"Relax, Leigh. We're just going to my backyard. I missed you after court."

"Wait a minute."

She dug in her heels and pulled them to a halt. He stopped and looked at her, wishing there was more light. The faint illumination from her porch light didn't reach this far. The starlight was too faint. He couldn't see her clearly. Her hair looked tousled, and her eyes were shining in the faint moonlight.

"Is there a problem with doing the unexpected?" he asked silkily.

"Do you do things like this often?" she asked her lips turning up into a smile.

"Never have done it before."

"A leopard can't change its spots," she murmured.

"Meaning?"

He leaned closer, breathing in the sweet fragrance she always wore. He wanted to do more than stand in the cool grass and argue about leopards.

"Meaning what are you up to?"

"I find I have a penchant for kidnapping. Maybe it's addictive."

"It's too late for a picnic."

"But not too late for dessert. Mrs. Norris made apple pie today. We can heat it up and top it with ice cream."

"It's after eleven."

Did her tone waver just a bit?

"Ah, too late for a swinging New Yorker like yourself?"

"Out of character for a staid attorney?"

"Ouch, is that how you see me?"

He pulled her closer. No man wanted to be thought of as staid. Unless maybe he was a hundred and three and couldn't move.

He wrapped his arms around her and kissed her long and deep. She made no struggle for freedom and Cooper took it for acquiescence. Teasing her lips, when she parted them, he plunged in to taste her sweetness.

To Leigh the world seemed to spin around. Cooper's touch ignited a blazing hot fire deep within. Her knees grew weak and desire rose wild and free. She loved the feel of him against her, loved the sensations that crowded, far too many to decipher. She didn't want the kiss to end. Eternity could come and go and she'd be satisfied to remain right here in Cooper's arms.

For an instant the thought bubbled up that he'd been reading Megan's diary as well. He certainly was acting in an unexpected manner. But she was too consumed with the passion that rose between them to question it. Time enough for that when she could think coherently.

Finally he ended the kiss, trailing soft kisses against her cheek, along her jaw, tilting her head back to kiss her neck, pausing on the rapid pulse point at the base of her throat.

He stood up and began to move again. When he reached his patio, he drew her up to one of the chairs and whispered, "Wait right here. I'll get the dessert and we'll have it out here."

She nodded, speech beyond her. When he let her go with another quick kiss, she swayed for a moment, then sank to the chair.

Pressing her fingers against her cheeks, she felt the warmth. What had Megan written? Something about understanding the man? Leigh now knew she hadn't a clue to who Cooper was, or what he was thinking.

Suddenly the game was on again and she was unsure of any of the rules. The only thing she was certain of was she'd never been kissed like that before. Even if she could stumble to her house, she wouldn't have moved an inch. She wanted to see what happened next.

The flagstones of the patio were warm beneath her feet, still retaining the heat from the sun.Sitting on one of the lounge chairs, she drew her knees up to her chest and covered her legs with her loose shirt.

It was a balmy, warm night. The lights from various houses in the neighborhood cast a soft glow. The moon was low on the horizon, almost full. Providing enough light to see by, now that her eyes had adjusted.

She remembered other Southern summer nights. A long time ago, when she'd first started visiting, she and Meredith and the Simmons boys had rousing games of hide and seek long after dark, roaming all over the neighborhood, playing with all the other teenagers who lived nearby. As she'd grown, she and Meredith spent time sharing confidences and dreams beneath the oak tree in the back of the yard—long after her aunt and uncle had retired for the evening.

"Apple pie à la mode."

Leigh reached up for the plate and fork. She straightened her legs, letting the T-shirt pool around her. Taking a bite, she smiled as the taste of apples, sugar and cinnamon exploded on her tongue.

"Ummm, delicious," she said, taking another bite. "Mrs. Norris still makes the best pie I've ever eaten."

Cooper sat in the chair beside her. For several moments they were silent as they savored the tasty dessert.

"Penny for your thoughts," he said, setting his empty plate on the flagstone.

"I was thinking about being a kid here, about all the fun we had after dark. You were too old to play hide and seek with us, but it was great. And then Uncle Paul used to barbeque. It was easier than heating up the kitchen, Aunt Lila always said. Now I wonder if it was just easier for her having him prepare dinner. But to me, it was magical. My folks get enough of meals outside on their digs that they don't find it appealing when they're home."

"Paul never seemed to mind cooking. They still barbeque several times a week in the summer. Some of the world's best chefs are men."

"Theirs is a good marriage, a blending of two lives that complement each other. And permit each other to do the things they like. My folks are a bit like that. Of course they both are consumed with archeology and anthropology, so that strengthens their tie."

"You're doing it again," he said looking up at the stars scattered across the dark sky.

"What?"

"Bringing up long-lasting marriages."

"Oh."

Leigh hadn't meant to be obvious. Should she say something about his parents being the exception? To what end?

"Maybe I want you to consider that marriage isn't such an antiquated institution. When I was thinking about it the other day, your parents are the only ones I know who separated. My friends still have their parents together, my folks and aunt and uncle…"

"So they are the exceptions."

"Or maybe your mom and dad were, did you ever think of that?"

When he remained silent for several minutes, Leigh could have bitten her tongue. Better just to keep quiet than try to change his mind.

"Why do you do that?" he asked.

"Do what? Bring up uncomfortable topics?"

"No, go silent sometimes. The Leigh I remember was a real chatterbox."

"The Leigh you remember was also very young. I'm grown up now, Cooper."

"With different life experiences. What was living in New York really like?"

"I told you the other evening."

"Not much. It seems to me I've dominated most of our conversations. You told me about your job on the phone and about some friends you have there. But nothing about men. Do you date a lot?"

Her pie finished, Leigh set her plate on the flagstone and lay back in the recliner, conscious of her scanty attire, of the fact she wore nothing beneath the T-shirt except her panties.

Yet it was dark. She could scarcely make out Cooper's silhouette against the night sky. He wouldn't be able to see anything. And it was fun to talk with him, share a bit of the past few years. How odd that he zeroed in on her romantic past. Not that she planned to tell him about it, or the lack thereof. She changed the subject.

"I really liked seeing you in court today," she said. "You looked formidable, yet came across that you were on the side of the witnesses. I expect you are really very good at what you do."

"It comes from years of experience, practice and some failures. But nothing comes without its price."

"And what price did you pay?" she asked.

Cooper thought about it for a few moments, then shifted on his chair, sitting up.

"Being single-minded in one's career doesn't leave a lot of time for other pursuits."

"Light on the social life?" she guessed, remembering how when she was in the throes of a big campaign she ruthlessly focused all her attention on the project to the detriment of her own social life.

In fact her entire stay in New York led to little in the way of activities that didn't complement her job.

"It certainly takes a backseat. You changed the subject—tell me about your social life."

"Not much to tell. I've got to go, Cooper. It's really late and I'm starting to get cold."

He rose and held out his hand to assist her. Leigh hesitated, then put hers into his. When his warm fingers covered hers, she caught her breath, her heart rate increasing again. Why did she have this reaction every time the man touched her? For goodness sakes, it was just Cooper Bryant.

"Next time I kidnap you, I'll do the blindfold bit," he murmured, drawing her close, putting his arms around her.

Leigh braced her arms against his chest, but couldn't resist the fluttering sensations that washed through her as he drew her tighter and tighter against his own hard body. And truth to be told, she didn't want to resist. Slowly she raised her face, and met his kiss.

Eons later, or was it only moments, he released her.

"Midnight madness," he murmured.

Chapter Seven

Midnight madness. Leigh nodded. It was as good a name as any for what had just happened. She turned and walked swiftly toward her aunt's home, thoughts and emotions and feelings all churning inside until she thought she'd go crazy. She was *not* going to fall for Cooper Bryant again.

But it was hard to convince herself when her body still tingled from being held by him. When she could still taste him on her lips. Maybe he'd changed. Maybe leopards *did* change their spots.

No, she shook her head to dispel the fantasy notion. By his age, he was firmly set in his ways. It'd take a miracle and a half to change the man.

And she was fresh out of miracles.

The dew was forming on the grass. Her feet were getting cold. And she couldn't believe she wore nothing but her nightshirt. Her aunt would be scandalized. Even her very liberated mother would probably raise an eyebrow at her attire.

"Good night, Leigh," he called when she reached the porch steps.

"Good night."

She dashed up the steps, pausing at the door. Looking at him over her shoulder, she impulsively blurted out an invitation.

"I'm making jambalaya on Saturday. Meredith and Josiah are

coming for dinner. Want to join us?"

She held her breath. If he said no, she'd invite Karl. But before the thought make itself known, he accepted.

"What time?"

"Sixish."

Committed, she entered the house and closed the door firmly behind her before she could do something foolish like turn around and fling herself into his arms. It would never do to show such an interest. Though what he thought of her after the way she responded to his kisses was beyond her. He had to know she'd unlikely turn him down.

And yet, maybe that was exactly what she should do.

Instead, she'd invited him for Saturday.

Shivering slightly from the night air, she hurried up to bed. But sleep was the farthest thing from her mind. Her blood hummed through her veins. Her skin tingled and her heart rate was still out of control.

Switching off the light, she tried to fall asleep, but it proved impossible. All she could do was remember his kiss, relive the touch of his skin against hers, his mouth moving, his tongue stroking, his hands molding her body to his.

Sitting up, she flicked the light back on and reached for Great-grandma Megan's journal. If she couldn't sleep for thinking about Cooper, time she took her mind off him.

Mama seems to have an old saying or old wives' tale for every event in life. Today she and I were preparing supper when she looked at me and winked. The way to a man's heart is through his stomach, she said. Daddy loves red-eyed gravy and so we were fixing one of his favorite meals that included gravy over rice. A happily fed man is content, and easy to be around, she added. So am I to cook for Frederick? I don't see when I can. Except for maybe the box social that's held on the Fourth of July. But that is months away. How can I show him what a good cook I am before then? I love getting all this advice from other women, but hate to let everyone know of my interest in Frederick. What if he never returns my regard?

I think Mama suspects, however. She said maybe I should think about preparing a Sunday dinner soon. We could invite the pastor and his wife. And maybe Frederick. She didn't say anything more. It's a good idea. But I've never known her to include anyone else when we have the pastor and his wife for Sunday dinner. I already know Frederick loves fried chicken. Cousin Biddy says I make the best fried chicken in the family. Wonder if Frederick will like it.

Leigh reread the passages she'd read that morning. Well, chalk up another one for Megan, she thought. Now if Cooper liked her jambalaya— Suddenly aware of where her thoughts were leading, Leigh tossed the journal aside and settled down to go to sleep. She'd think of how hard she'd worked in New York, of where she wanted to find another job, of what she'd wear on Saturday night.

Leigh went shopping Friday morning for the ingredients for jambalaya.

She spent the afternoon cleaning the house, though she planned for dinner to be served on the patio. Still, it was nice to mindlessly do tasks at her own pace. She'd quickly bounced back from her feeling of listlessness after working so hard all winter and spring. In fact, she was beginning to get a little restless.

Monday, she'd seriously begin to look for a job.

And maybe check out apartments in the Charlotte area. If she found something soon, she'd make a quick trip to New York to pack and arrange to ship her furniture and belongings south.

Maybe Meredith would take a few days off and come with her. They could take in a Broadway show and she could show off New York to her cousin before heading back.

Saturday dawned hot and humid. Leigh prepared the

jambalaya early, wanting it to simmer all day to blend the flavors. She planned to serve a fresh mixed green salad and hot cornbread with pineapple upside-down cake for dessert. It was her her aunt's recipe and everyone loved it.

If she recalled correctly, it had been a favorite of Cooper's. She remembered him stopping by when she was younger and eating huge pieces of her aunt's cake.

Hearing a lawn mower some time later, Leigh glanced out the window. Cooper was cutting his lawn. Fascinated by the man he'd become, she watched for several long moments. He wore those ragged cutoffs and tatty old tennis shoes. The sun gleamed on his skin—his shoulders and chest muscular and solid looking. The dark tan was still surprising so early in the summer, yet if he did all his yard work without a shirt, that explained it.

Oblivious to everything but the task at hand, he never glanced her way. Gratefully, Leigh watched until he moved to the front yard. Sighing softly, she returned to her cooking. If she didn't watch herself that crush she'd once had so badly would resurface and she'd be in a pickle.

She should have invited Karl tonight. Or not listened to Meredith and kept her guest list to her cousin and Josiah. The three of them had enjoyed dinner last week. They didn't need a fourth.

Too late now to change anything. But she'd keep the evening casual. Three old friends and Josiah.

Leigh was debating whether to slip out to the country club for a quick dip in the pool that afternoon when the phone rang. She'd like to swim, but knew the pool would likely be crowded with families and children. Still, it would be nice to cool off and work on her tan a bit more. Her days of being a lady of leisure were fast waning.

"Hello?"

"Leigh?" a familiar voice croaked.

"Meredith? What's wrong? You sound terrible."

"I feel even worse! I have the most awful cold. I can't believe I got one this time of year. I'm so miserable. I can't come to dinner tonight. I called Josiah and told him already."

"But you have to come. I have a ton of food. And I already invited Cooper."

"Even if I could crawl out of bed, I wouldn't want to infect everyone. You and Cooper have dinner. Freeze what you don't eat and we can have it next week when I'm feeling better. If I ever feel better."

"Colds don't last that long, you'll be fine in a couple of days."

Leigh's heart sank. She'd been counting on her cousin and Josiah to be there. Would Cooper believe they'd been invited when they didn't show up? He'd probably think it was some ploy by Leigh to have him over.

"Maybe, but right now I feel terrible. I'd much rather it be cool and raining outside than have this cold when the weather's so beautiful," Meredith complained.

"Drink a lot of fluids—"

Meredith laughed, then coughed.

"Now you sound like Mom. I'll take care of myself. Have fun tonight, sorry I'll miss it. But I wouldn't even be able to taste anything feeling like this."

Tonight? There was no way she was going to entertain Cooper alone. Leigh hung up and looked out the window. No sign of Cooper. The lawn mower had stopped long ago. Was he inside? Should she call him and cancel? It was one thing to have him over when there were others. Something else again if it were just the two of them.

Going to the phone, she quickly dialed.

After four rings the answering machine responded.

"Hi Cooper, it's Leigh. Meredith is sick, so can't make dinner tonight. I guess we'd better cancel. I have a ton of food, though, so I can make you a plate if you like."

She frowned. If she were going to feed the man, why not have him eat at her place.

"Or you can still come over if you want, but Josiah and Meredith won't be here. It'll just be you and me."

Obviously.

She felt like an idiot. Would he think she was coming on to him?

"Or you can take it home."

Now she sounded like a take-out place.

"Call me," she ended and hung up before she said anything else stupid.

Looking out the front window, Leigh saw Cooper's car was gone. He'd get her message when he returned.

By five-thirty, she hadn't heard from him. Nor was his car in the driveway. Where was he, she wondered. Should she expect him at six or not?

The blue dress she wore was short and breezy. The sandals barely shod her feet and she'd splurged and painted her toenails a pale pink. The color looked nice against her newly acquired tan.

Entering the kitchen, she made the cornbread batter, poured it into the pan and set it near the stove. Quickly tossing a salad, she placed it in the refrigerator. She had to eat, even if Cooper didn't show up.

And if he did show, once he learned that Meredith and Josiah weren't here, he might wish to take a plate home and not bother making small talk while they ate.

Pacing the kitchen, she kept looking out the window. Where was he? Had he received her message?

When six o'clock came with no Cooper, Leigh knew he wasn't coming. He'd probably called his phone for messages from wherever he'd gone that day.

She'd pop the cornbread pan into the oven and eat when it was done. She wasn't really disappointed. It might have proved awkward to entertain him after last night's kisses.

Sighing softly, she checked on the cornbread. She'd be eating early. She'd planned to have a glass or two of wine on the patio before cooking the bread and serving the meal. But that's when she expected guests. Now she was on her own.

Retrieving Megan's diary, Leigh sat at the kitchen table reading it while the cornbread baked. The fragrance filled the room and her mouth watered. She didn't mind eating early, she was hungry.

The knock on the back door startled her. Cooper stood on the small porch, dressed in casual slacks and a pullover knit shirt in deep green.

"Sorry I'm late. I got held up."

"I didn't expect you," she said noting how handsome he looked.

Suddenly she remembered how great he'd looked earlier when cutting the lawn. There was no getting around the fact he was a fine figure of a man, as Megan would have said.

He looked at her quizzically.

"You said sixish. I know it's fifteen after, but surely that's close enough. Are you going to let me in?"

Flustered, she nodded and stepped back.

"Smells good," he said, looking around. "Where are Meredith and Josiah?"

"I left a message on your answering machine. Meredith's sick, so she canceled for them both. I called this morning, tried to reach you."

"I didn't even stop to check the machine. Sorry to hear she's sick. Is it bad?"

"Just a summer cold, though she feels miserable. But since it's just the two of us now, I thought maybe you'd rather not."

"I think we can muddle through a meal together, don't you?" he said.

Slowly he let his gaze skim across her shoulders, down the length of her body, stopping when he saw the polish on her toes. His mouth quirked up.

"Sure. Want a glass of wine?"

Leigh turned away before her knees gave way. The look he gave her was hot enough to melt iron.

"I had planned to sit outside and have dinner around seven, but I've already put in the cornbread. It'll be ready in a few more minutes."

"That's fine with me. I missed lunch. Had an appointment."

So that's why he was late. Why had he even agreed to come to dinner? She almost groaned aloud. She hadn't followed her great-grandmother's tenet about not being so readily available. She shouldn't have invited him.

Oh, no? her subconscious challenged.

"You could have called and canceled tonight," she said, relieved her voice sounded normal.

Pasting a bright smile on her face, she turned to hand him a glass of wine.

Cooper was leafing through the journal.

"Oh no, don't read that."

She dashed across the wide kitchen and thrust the wine glass at him, reaching to snatch away the journal at the same time. The last thing she wanted was for him to realize what she'd been doing since she arrived. He'd instantly suspect she was trying to lure him into some commitment trap. Given their history, he'd never believe she was just passing the time until the real Mr. Right appeared on the horizon.

He frowned, took the glass and looked at the leather-bound journal.

"A diary of some kind?" he asked.

She nodded.

"Meredith and Aunt Lila found it when cleaning out the attic this spring. From our great-grandmother. Mine and Meredith's I mean. It was from Aunt Lila's and Mom's grandmother. Their mother's mother."

She knew she was babbling, but couldn't stop.

"From when she was a child?"

"Not exactly. Actually it was from the day she turned eighteen. Back in those days that was considered all grown up. She writes about the family and about court—ah, I mean cotillions and things like that."

Turning away, she placed the journal on top of the refrigerator and peeked into the oven. The cornbread was a golden brown.

"Dinner's ready," she said. "Want to eat outside?"

Settled on the patio a few minutes later, Leigh was pleased to see Cooper enjoy the meal. She, on the other hand, could scarcely eat. She pushed some of the food around, took a small bite of jambalaya. Nervous, she picked at her salad.

"Something wrong?" Cooper asked watching her.

"No."

She smiled brightly, not quite meeting his eyes. Reaching for her wineglass, she took a sip, wishing now that she'd served iced tea.

"Did you have a nice afternoon?"

Leigh closed her eyes in disgust. The last thing she wanted to hear was about Cooper's day. How could she have said that? Bravely studying her plate she hoped Cooper thought she was making small talk. Not that she really cared how he spent his time. Or with whom.

"Nice? Wasn't that kind of appointment," he said, buttering a thick wedge of cornbread.

"What kind?"

"The kind where you have fun."

Leigh frowned.

"What kind did you have, then?"

"A business appointment, what did you think? A meeting with a private investigator for the case I'm working on." His eyes gleamed. "Did you think I left a hot date with another woman to join you for dinner?"

"I'd never think that," she retorted, feeling the heat steal into her cheeks.

She was glad mind reading wasn't his specialty. Or was it? The smug look on his face made her want to knock it off. He did think she was jealous. She'd have to prove to him that she couldn't care less.

"I saw you cut the grass this morning," she said, then remembered how she'd watched him from the window.

Maybe this wasn't the topic she wanted brought up.

"I thought you'd hire a gardener."

"I had one a few years ago, when Dad first sold me the house. But one day the man couldn't make it, so I did the work and found

I liked it. Having to do it as a teenager seemed a chore. Now that the place is mine, I feel differently about it. And mowing gives me time to think. There's also a surprising sense of satisfaction when I'm all done."

"I like gardening for the same reason. I hope I can have a balcony or something in my new apartment so I can grow flowers. I had a window box in New York, but that's all. Some day I'd like a huge old house where I could garden to my heart's content."

"New apartment?"

Trust him to pick up on that.

"Umm." She met his gaze, wondering what his thoughts were. "I'm going to see if I can obtain a job in Charlotte. Then I'd need a place to stay."

Cooper studied her thoughtfully.

"What's wrong with staying here in Willow Creek? I commute. It's not that far."

She shrugged.

"I think I'd like Charlotte. It's got more going for it than Willow Creek."

"Too quiet here for you?"

Toying with her wineglass, Leigh tried to find the words to explain what she was feeling. She didn't want to get into an argument with the man, but she had her own needs to consider.

"Actually, I think Willow Creek is a wonderful place to live. To raise a family." She met his eyes. "But until I do get married and get ready to start that family, I would rather be where there's more action."

And away from temptation in the form of a tall, sexy, dark-haired man.

"So you can pick up some guy?".

"Pick up? I don't think so. But meet, date. Not everyone's like you. I do want to find a mate, build a life together, share experiences with someone special."

"Marriage only gives the illusion of longevity. Depend on yourself, Leigh. You'll be less likely to be hurt that way."

"Cynic," she murmured.

"Realist, I believe. Where you're like Pollyanna, always seeing the best."

"Nothing wrong with that. There are a lot of people who have very wonderful marriages. Do you think I should cultivate cynicism like you?"

"No."

The clipped tone virtually ended the discussion.

Sipping from her wineglass, Leigh was puzzled. She'd almost think Cooper cared about her dating someone else, except the notion was too outlandish.

The silence stretched out for a long time. Finally, Cooper laid down his fork.

"The meal was delicious, Leigh," he said formally.

"Thanks. I have pineapple upside-down cake for dessert, want any?"

"Your aunt's recipe?"

"What other one would I use? I know you like this one."

"Ah, did you bake this cake for me?"

Flustered, Leigh stacked their plates and rose, heading toward the kitchen. She glanced over her shoulder and shook her head.

"Meredith and I like it, too. And I thought Josiah would as well."

Cooper rose and followed her into the kitchen.

"I'm glad you made it, whatever the reason."

Leigh had placed the cake in the oven to warm with the residual heat from baking the cornbread. She withdrew it and cut generous portions.

"Ice cream on the side?" she asked, wishing he'd remained outside.

He seemed to fill the kitchen, crowd her, though there was plenty of room. But he stepped closer and she almost panicked.

"Of course."

Cooper reached into the freezer and withdrew the carton of ice cream.

"Shall I scoop it up?"

She nodded, moving away from the plates. He seemed to take up all the air. And she wasn't sure how her equilibrium would survive in such close proximity.

But for a moment fantasy took possession of her mind. She could almost imagine being married to Cooper, sharing tasks in the kitchen, preparing meals together, and discussing their day.

Turning her head swiftly, she could almost hear the patter of little feet running toward them. Foolish thoughts. Hadn't Cooper made it clear a hundred times he was not interested in the institution of marriage?

Settled back on the patio a few minutes later, Leigh was pleased at the way Cooper enjoyed the cake. It tasted as good as any her aunt baked. In fact, the entire evening was going better than she had hoped when Meredith canceled.

Cooper took the last bite of his cake and then leaned back in the chair.

"Dinner was delicious, Leigh. You're a good cook."

"Thank you."

He watched her as she finished eating. Her cooking ability surprised him. Somehow he still thought of Leigh as the obnoxious teenager who followed him around like he was some superhero.

Logically he realized that she'd grown up, moved beyond that. She'd spent years in New York. Built a successful career. Just because it got sidetracked by the takeover didn't mean she wouldn't land on her feet. He was growing to know this new Leigh, and found himself intrigued by the different facets she revealed.

And the differences from his preconceived ideas. It was dangerous in his line of work to become fixed on any one idea. He needed to view things with openness, be aware of changes and clues that gave him insight into people. He didn't seem to be doing such a great job with Leigh.

Intrigued and perplexed was how he felt. He wouldn't have expected this sophisticated woman across from him.

He still looked for traces of that younger Leigh who had so adored him.

What kind of person did it make him that he now missed that adoration? He didn't deserve any of it. He'd virtually ignored her existence for the last several years. Now that her devotion was missing, he wanted it. At least some form of it.

He wasn't sure he liked her idea of moving to Charlotte. Granted, she'd lived farther away when in New York, but now that he'd seen her again, discovered they could spend time together without her throwing herself at him, he liked it. He felt comfortable around Leigh. They both knew the score, so there were no machinations trying to entrap him.

"You haven't mentioned Samuel. What's he up to these days?" she asked, referring to his brother.

"He lives in Los Angeles, works for an aerospace firm out there."

"Is he married?"

"No."

He heard her soft sigh.

"That's too bad."

"Not necessarily."

Cooper could feel himself tighten at the trend of the conversation. Did she constantly bring up marriage? Or was it his own heightened awareness of the institution that made it seem a favorite topic of conversation?

"There are lots of happy marriages in the world. Why shouldn't Samuel have one? Or you for that matter?" Leigh said gently.

"There are many that are unhappy. What then? What if you have children and then can't stand the way your life turned out. It's unfair to dump that on children."

"It'd be devastating. Is that how you felt when your mom left? Devastated?"

"We're not talking about me or my family."

"I think we are. It's colored your entire view of family life. That and the woman in college."

Cooper stared at her. Leaning forward, his eyes caught hers, held.

"What do you know about a woman in college?" he asked, his tone deadly.

Leigh sat up and glared back.

"Don't try to intimidate me, Mr. Hotshot Attorney. I knew you when you'd get all dirty practicing football and Mrs. Norris would yell at you to keep your muddy footprints off her clean kitchen floor. And I'm not some witness to be interrogated."

"Leigh," his tone held a warning.

What had she heard about Celia? And from whom?

She dropped her gaze, and traced a pattern on the edge of the table.

"I heard that you fell in love and the woman dumped you."

Cooper almost winced. He waited for the crashing pain of betrayal, the sharp edge of bitter unhappiness. Startled, he found there was none. Celia had mattered so much to an impressionable young man that he thought he'd suffer from her defection forever.

Now he had trouble even remembering what she looked like. Had her hair been medium brown, or darker? What color were her eyes?

He had no trouble envisioning Leigh, even when they'd been apart for a long time. Her light brown hair had golden highlights that drew the eye. Her dark brown eyes changed with her emotions. Suddenly Cooper wondered what they would look like when she was making love. Would they glow with inner fire?

He hadn't paid attention to her eyes when he'd kissed her. He'd been too absorbed in the feelings that exploded every time his mouth melded with hers. Too caught up in the feel of her tantalizing body pressed against his, too captivated by the sweet taste of her. Too enthralled with the sound of her soft reactions to his kisses. Next time he'd look into her eyes and see what happened.

Next time?

"It's none of your business," he said.

"Maybe not, but it sure had an impact on your life. But not everyone is like your mother or Celia. You surely aren't expecting to live your life alone. Don't you sometimes wish there was a special someone to share momentous events with? I sure do. I had lots of friends in New York, but whenever I got a promotion, or a new assignment, I called home to share with those who genuinely love me. Who loves *you,* Cooper?"

He drew in a sharp breath. She was cutting too close to the bone, now.

"I don't *need* anyone to love me, Leigh. That emotion is a myth, an illusion that people use to cover lust. It makes it sound so much better to sleep with someone if you're *in love*. But the fact is there's no such thing as a lasting love. You only have to look at my mother to see that. Even if she stopped caring for my father, what about her two sons?"

"I don't know. Do you have the full story behind that breakup? You were a little boy. And my aunt said your father changed after that. She knew them both, liked them both. Maybe she did try to see you and your dad wouldn't let her. Or maybe not. Whatever, it happened a long time ago. And why give her that much power if you don't like her? The power to keep you from finding someone who cares about you, who wants what's best for you—however you define that. Someone who would share her life with you. Let go of the past, Cooper. Reach for the future."

"Shouldn't we learn from our experiences?"

"I think love is a strong bond between people. I love my parents and they love me. They adore each other. My dad would walk through fire for my mom, and I want to find that kind of love for myself. I don't want to be alone all my life. I want a special person to share it with."

She jumped up.

"But that's not you."

Reaching for his plate, she leaned over a bit and glared at him.

"You're going to regret it when you are old and gray and can't work and there's no one around to remember the old days with you. Do you want to take some cake home with you?"

Cooper almost laughed at her abrupt change. Almost, but not quite. He wanted to be angry at her tirade, but there was a glimmer of truth in her words.

"If you can spare a piece," he replied evenly.

"I certainly can. If it's around I'll eat it and I don't need the extra calories."

He watched her sweep into the kitchen. For a moment he wanted to follow her, but reconsidered. He'd stated his position. She'd stated hers. Stalemate.

Neither believed the other's stance appropriate. He just hoped she didn't end up in a marriage that made her miserable. Or walk away from her children in ten years.

The thought of Leigh getting married nagged at him. Frowning, he tried to put the thought out of his mind. But he could envision her walking down the aisle at the Baptist church, escorted by her father, wearing some extravagant, beautiful white wedding gown. Pledging herself to some faceless man.

Clenching his fists, Cooper wondered if the man would be good to her. No matter what, Leigh had been part of his childhood, and he didn't want any harm to come to her.

Rising, he started toward the house when she came out, carefully carrying a covered plate.

"Here it is. Don't eat it all at once."

Her smile was friendly. Her eyes clear. There was no subterfuge with this woman.

"It's a wonderful cake. I'll enjoy every bite," he said taking the plate.

"Sorry Meredith and Josiah didn't make it. Maybe another time."

She backed up a step.

With a hint of mischief, Cooper stepped forward. Leigh moved back another pace. Reaching out with his free hand, he caught the nape of her neck and gently pulled her closer.

"I have to get the dishes done," she said breathlessly.

"They can wait. Is this good-night?"

She fidgeted beneath his gaze. Was she nervous? Of him? Not likely after blasting him a few minutes ago.

When she looked up, her eyes were uncertain. Remembering what he wanted to know, he kissed her. Her lips parted and she responded perfectly. Pulling back a bit, Cooper stared into her warm eyes, burning with inner fire.

He wanted her. Stunned at the revelation, he couldn't think. The schoolgirl from his younger years had metamorphosed into a beautiful, compelling woman. One he wanted to know in every way possible. When had this happened? What had Leigh done to change? Or had he been the one to change?

Her hair skimmed across the back of his fingers. He could feel the warmth of her body as she stood so close, yet not quite touching. He wanted more. More than mere kisses. He wanted all of her.

Chapter Eight

"Good night, Cooper," Leigh said, slipping from beneath his hand.

She was scarcely breathing. She had to get away before she made a total fool of herself over this man.

"Leigh, wait."

"I've got to go. Bye."

She scooted the short distance to the kitchen door and flew inside, letting the screen slam behind her.

Taking a deep breath she wondered what she was doing. Arguing for the institution of marriage with a man who was dead set against it was an exercise in futility.

And caring for such a man would be a dumb move. Really dumb. Hadn't she learned anything in life? Tilting at windmills got her nowhere.

She'd done her utmost to stem the tide when the takeover came. It had accomplished nothing except wear her out.

As would caring for Cooper.

Almost afraid Cooper would follow her into the kitchen, she went to the sink and began to do the dishes. It didn't take long. Once done, she peered out into the darkened yard. He was gone. Thank goodness.

"A narrow escape. If he kept kissing me, I'd forget every

lonely day since he so scathingly turned on me and fall back in love with the man," she whispered into the night.

Horrified with the trend of her thoughts, she shook her head. No way was she going to fall in love with a man who wanted nothing to do with her.

Time she started looking for that new job. And a new place to live that wasn't right next door to Cooper. Get herself so busy with other things she didn't have a minute to think about what might have been.

The phone rang.

"Hello?"

"Thanks again for dinner," the familiar, sexy voice said.

Leigh shivered and sank onto the chair. Maybe if she recorded his voice, she could play it over and over until she got so sick of hearing it, she'd become immune to its attraction.

"I'm glad you enjoyed it. I don't get to cook often and I like to."

"You can cook for me anytime."

She smiled, thinking of Megan's advice. Would that breach the walls around his heart?

"I think Mrs. Norris would object. She'd think I was usurping her place."

"If you repeat what I'm about to say, I'll deny it all the way to the Supreme Court, but your cooking is much better than hers."

The warmth of his compliment washed through her.

"Thanks. I'm glad you enjoyed it, but that's just based on one meal. You'd be better off staying with Mrs. Norris."

"Have dinner with me tomorrow night?"

She gripped the receiver. Two nights in a row? She almost said yes, then remembered Megan's words of wisdom.

"Sorry, I'm busy."

"Doing what?" he asked quickly.

"You know, Cooper, you need to watch that habit of cross-examining everyone you come in contact with. As you said when I mentioned Celia, it's none of your business."

"Monday night?"

Leigh suspected by the sound of his voice he wasn't used to being turned down. Perversity reared its head.

"Nope, sorry."

She almost laughed, waiting anxiously to see if he'd counter.

"Tuesday?"

Biting her lower lip to keep from laughing, she remained silent wondering just how far he'd push? Did he really want to see her again, or was it a case of pushing until he got what he wanted?

"Wednesday then. In fact, I'll take you around to some of the apartment complexes in Charlotte Wednesday afternoon. I already know I won't be in court. We can get dinner afterward."

"Why would you want to help me apartment hunt?" she asked, surprised by the offer.

"Who better to advise you on the lease parameters than an attorney?"

Warily, Leigh agreed.

"Wednesday, then. About one?"

"Shall I pick you up?"

"No, I'll come into town. No sense you driving out here and then back."

"Get home early Tuesday so you're not tired."

"What are you, my new father?"

"No, Leigh, but if you're busy every night until Wednesday, I suspect you'll be exhausted."

"I'll just sleep in late every morning," she said, almost laughing again.

She had nothing planned for any evening, but she wouldn't tell Cooper that. Let him think she was in high demand. Did it raise her worth in his eyes? She frowned. She wished to be wanted for herself, not because he thought she was some prize to be won.

Taking the journal upstairs after Cooper hung up, Leigh planned to read until she fell asleep. The dinner had turned out unexpectedly well, but she wished Meredith and Josiah had been able to attend. She'd have learned more about her neighbor if he and Josiah had exchanged reminiscences.

Then her thoughts veered toward Wednesday.

She couldn't imagine Cooper arranging to take time from work to help her do anything eleven years ago. Couldn't imagine him kissing her, either. She'd tried that once, with disastrous results. But there was nothing wrong with his kisses now. They were simply wonderful.

"Forget it, he's not for you," she admonished herself firmly.

But as she stared at the list of ideas her great-grandmother had written down in her youthful exuberance, Leigh shivered, wondering if they alone were responsible for the change in the way Cooper acted.

"You should have published them, if they really work," Leigh murmured, slowly turning the pages already read.

Did they work with everyone? She needed to meet a man she felt she could connect with and try them again to prove their worth. Maybe the move to Charlotte was the best thing. She'd have a new circle of friends and find the opportunity to meet nice eligible men.

Not that Cooper wasn't nice. She almost cringed. Somehow the term sounded too insipid when referring to him. Dangerous, intriguing, sexy—all more powerful terms to describe the man.

But eligible would never apply. Not unless he made a major change.

Leigh purposefully avoided Cooper during the first part of the week. She made sure she was inside before he arrived home each evening, not sitting on the front porch until long after dark, when he couldn't see her.

Tuesday evening, she went to Meredith's. Her cousin was feeling much better, and they cooked on a small grill on Meredith's balcony. Sitting at the tiny table to eat, Leigh mentioned Cooper planned to take her apartment hunting. Meredith frowned.

"Why?"

"Said he'd look over the leases for me," Leigh said, trying for a nonchalant attitude.

Sipping her iced tea, she gazed over the grass of the apartment complex in which Meredith lived, avoiding her cousin's gaze lest she guess Leigh truly didn't feel that nonchalance.

"He seems a lot more attentive than he used to. In fact, it's almost a complete turnaround, don't you think?" Meredith considered her cousin for a moment. "Watch yourself, I wouldn't trust him for a minute."

"He's your parents' next-door neighbor, nothing more," Leigh said, hoping her cousin couldn't detect the uncertainty in her voice.

Cooper was growing more important to her every time they met. She'd thought herself immune to his charm, to the attraction that she'd used to feel for him. She'd been convinced his scathing denouncement years ago had cured her of any feelings.

She'd been wrong. Each minute they spent together only brought a bit more uncertainty. And flared the attraction that had never really died.

If she didn't want to lose her heart to the man, she'd better start looking elsewhere for companionship.

"Just be careful. You know he has no interest in a long-term commitment."

"I know. If I get an apartment in Charlotte, I'll be far away from temptation."

"Aha, so you feel there *is* temptation with Cooper?"

"Have you ever looked at the man? He's a walking testament to masculine perfection."

She closed her eyes briefly, seeing his tall, lean body, his wide shoulders, remembering the defined muscles when he mowed his lawn. She sighed softly.

Meredith laughed.

"Leigh, you have it bad. I personally think Josiah is a walking testament to masculine perfection and I'm crazy about the man. I thought you got over your crush on Cooper years ago."

"I did. I know better than to fall for Cooper. Let's change the subject. I have something else I wanted to ask you. Did Megan marry Frederick?"

"What?"

"The journal tells me how she's enticing the man by doing all these different tactics—like being unavailable, cooking his favorite meals. I've only read some of the journal and so far it's taken place over several months. Did she and Frederick marry?"

"I don't know."

"You don't know? I thought you said you'd skimmed through the journal."

"I skimmed through it here and there, read the first few pages and the last few pages. It covered several years altogether. I didn't think I needed to read it closely. And Mom really wanted to read it."

"What was Megan's last name?"

Meredith sighed, "I don't know that either. She died when we were young. I always called her Great-grandma Megan."

"Me, too. You'd think someone would have mentioned her last name. Or our great-grandfather's name."

"She was our mothers' grandmother. Her daughter was their mother. I don't know if I ever heard her last name. And he died before we were born. I guess there just wasn't any need to mention him by the time we came along. We can ask Mom."

"By the time they get back I'll be through the journal."

"Well, read ahead and find out."

Leigh shook her head.

"I don't want to do that. But I sure hope she married her Frederick. She seems so in love with him. And she's doing her best to follow all the advice her mother and aunts are giving her. Some of it seems to work. How could we know so little about our family?"

"Ask your mother. I expect with her interest in anthropology, she also knows everything there is to know about the family."

"Maybe, I haven't been all that interested before. But after reading Megan's diary, I feel as if I know her. And for all the decades that separate us, she's a young woman on the threshold of the rest of her life—which is how I look at myself."

"A bit older than she was," Meredith murmured.

"Yes, but just as interested in her plans as any of her friends might be."

"What do you mean?"

"I'm doing the same thing, and—"

Leigh stopped as an idea hit her.

She looked at Meredith with consideration. It'd be perfect.

"Meredith, if I give you some pointers, would you try them and then tell me the results?"

"What is this, some kind of experiment?"

"Sort of."

Leigh explained her idea—for Meredith to try Great-grandma Megan's advice on Josiah to see if she noticed any change in the man and their relationship. Wringing a reluctant agreement from her cousin, Leigh soon left for home.

She'd have to write down all the different ideas and give them to Meredith. Once her cousin tried them with Josiah, Leigh'd have a better feeling about if they really worked.

Were they sound ideas, or was it just serendipity that it seemed to be working with Cooper. Not that he'd done or said anything to lead her to believe he was looking for a long-term relationship. But the times they'd been together were well worth the small effort she had made.

She liked wearing flowing dresses, delighted in their picnic, enjoyed cooking. Was it all that simple? Do what you like without artificial posturing and see what happens?

When the receptionist announced Leigh's arrival on Wednesday afternoon, Cooper felt a sense of relief—he'd been worried she wouldn't show. He hadn't seen her since their dinner on Saturday night. And been surprised to find over the last few days that he missed her.

"Hello, Cooper."

Leigh breezed into his office with a bright smile on her face. He felt the impact like a kick. She looked beautiful, and so happy it almost hurt to look at her.

The dress she wore emphasized her slender curves. The pale peach color was perfect with the deepening tan on her shoulders and arms. He wished he could spend time with her when she was in the sun. He'd like to see her long legs gleaming with oil, observe how her swimsuit covered that slender body, yet revealed her soft curves and valleys.

"No kidnapping today?"

He'd better think of other things before he embarrassed them both, he thought as he rose and crossed his office to greet her. It seemed natural to kiss her. His hands covered her arms, and he drew her closer. It was briefer than he wanted, but permitted him to set the tone of the afternoon.

She blinked and shook her head, tilting it to one side as she smiled at him.

"Not today. Be on your guard, you never know when the kidnapper might strike again."

Feeling ten feet tall at the rising color in her cheeks, a clear reaction to his kiss, Cooper reached for his suit jacket and shrugged it on, all the time watching her. Was it his imagination or did his office suddenly seem brighter?

He glanced over his shoulder at the window. The sun had been shining all day. It made no sense that it was brighter now.

"Did you eat?"

"Yes. Did you?"

"I grabbed a sandwich. I have a list of places on the West side that are in good neighborhoods. You didn't mention your price range, but these are moderate," Cooper said, handing her a computer printout from the corner of the desk.

"I didn't expect all this," she said, scanning the list. "I brought the paper. I read all the ads this morning and circled a couple that looked appealing."

"Maybe we can find something today," he said, ushering her out.

But only if it was perfect. It wouldn't hurt her to remain in Willow Creek a bit longer. Long enough for him to get her out of his system, at least.

The first apartment had already been rented. But the second looked promising to Leigh. She followed the manager through a winding walkway lined on both sides with neatly trimmed shrubbery. The grassy area was small, but neatly cut. Flowers dotted the landscape providing colorful spots of color against the deep green expanse.

"Two bedroom, but the price is real competitive," the manager said as she opened the door and stood aside for Leigh and Cooper to enter.

"You two take your time. I'll wait here."

Smiling, the woman turned to look over the grounds.

Leigh walked around the living room. It seemed small after her aunt's spacious house, but was larger than her apartment in New York. There was a small patio area beyond sliding glass doors. She walked over, wondering if she could put planter boxes there. It was in the shade now, but maybe it received morning sun.

"It's a bit small," Cooper said.

She turned around.

"Not for an apartment. My place in New York is smaller than this and I was lucky to get it. You're spoiled, living in that big old house."

He raised an eyebrow but remained silent.

Leigh walked down the short hall to the first bedroom. It was tiny, with a window high in the opposite wall. Moving to the next room, she knew it was the master bedroom. It was a bit larger and had an adjacent bath. Like the first bedroom, it only had a single window high in the wall. The room was rather dim, but it didn't matter if all she planned to do in it was sleep.

"Let's check the kitchen," she said, turning.

She almost bumped into Cooper. He studied the room for a minute, then looked at her.

"I don't like it," he said. "It's dark and small. You wouldn't like it here."

"I like the living room. If the kitchen is adequate, it would be a possibility. But I would want to see the others first."

By the time the afternoon drew to a close, Leigh was no closer to finding a place than she had been that morning, and about ready to scream in frustration. Cooper had criticized every place they'd seen. Either the apartment was too small, or did not provide enough security, or was in the path of too much traffic, too noisy, too old. His criticisms never ceased.

When they pulled away from the last building, Leigh glared at him.

"This was a waste of time. You insulted that manager worse than the others."

"I insulted no one. If he can't stand to hear a few home truths about the neglect around the place, he shouldn't have let things fall apart. This is the worst of the bunch."

"I liked the first one we saw and that one on Rose Street."

"You wouldn't be happy in either," he stated.

"You'd be surprised what I can be happy in. I'd fix it up so it was perfect for me. And the price of that one on Rose Street is attractive."

"Probably hiding dry rot or a leaking roof, it was so cheap."

Leigh sighed, holding on to her temper by a thread.

"You know, Cooper, I don't think this was such a good idea."

"What?" he asked, maneuvering in the heavy rush-hour traffic.

"Your coming with me. You've never had to find an apartment. They're different from houses. I can't expect the same kind of amenities a house offers."

He frowned.

"I had an apartment in college."

"Then think back, what was it like?"

"Small, noisy and crowded, just like half the ones we saw today. They won't do, Leigh."

She looked out of the window. It was a lost cause. Next time she'd go apartment hunting alone. In fact, she might drive back to the one on Rose Street in the morning and see if she still liked it. Cooper had no real say in her life. If she still wanted that apartment when she saw it again, she'd take it.

Leigh glanced at Cooper.

"At least your house now is totally different from your apartment. You have all those rooms and live there alone. It is large, quiet and empty."

He frowned.

"It's home."

"Do you ever get lonely?"

"Do you?"

"I did when I first moved to New York. And even sometimes after I'd been there a while. But now that I'm back, I haven't been once. Meredith is close enough we can see each other whenever we want. We talk on the phone almost every day. I've been seeing other friends. There's something special about being with people who have known me since I was a little girl that's missing with friends in New York. I'll miss them when I move, but I think coming to Charlotte will be the best thing for me."

Cooper turned into the parking lot beside a large restaurant.

"Italian all right with you?" he asked.

"Yes, sounds wonderful. I'm hungry."

They were soon seated in a quiet booth. Cooper ordered a carafe of red wine, then waited for Leigh to decide what she wished to eat before placing their orders.

She smiled at him and raised her glass. "

Thanks anyway for today."

"I don't think any of the apartments were any good for you."

"But that has to be my decision, right? You chose that huge house. What do you do in it, sleep in a different bedroom every night? You should have a large family to fill it up."

He shook his head.

"Never happen."

"You never want children?"

"No."

"You'd make a great father, I bet," she said.

Cooper hesitated a moment, studying the wine the steward had poured into his glass. If he were honest, he'd admit to wishing for a son or daughter.

"The risk is too high," he said slowly.

"What risk?"

His gaze met hers.

"The risk of a failed marriage, of a woman deserting her children."

"All life is a risk. Your wife could be killed. You could be killed by a runaway truck tomorrow. There are no guarantees," Leigh said softly, her heart aching for him. "And why are you always looking on the worst-case scenario? What if she didn't leave? What if your marriage didn't fail, but ended up lasting for over fifty years?"

She wished he'd be willing to try. She'd never leave him. If he married her, there would be no risk.

Appalled at the thought, she swiftly reached for her glass. She was not even in the running for Cooper Bryant.

"Maybe I need to find someone like you used to be. Someone who thinks I hung the moon."

"If you ever do, don't turn on her and kill that adoration. It hurt," she said softly, remembering.

"I never meant to hurt you," Cooper said.

"You meant to do whatever would discourage me." She shrugged. "Water long under the bridge. Ah, garlic bread and salad. I love Italian food. This was a good choice."

The conversation moved to strictly impersonal from Leigh's side. She had danced too close to the flames to feel comfortable discussing Cooper's solitary state. He'd had a chance years ago and thrown it away. She wasn't in the running any more.

Cooper knew the subject of children had been closed, but he couldn't discount the idea now that she'd brought it up. What would it be like to be a father? He knew he wouldn't repeat the mistakes of his own father. But would he make others, equally wrong? Would he rear a child who didn't feel strongly about him? His father had essentially left the same time as his mother, only his body had remained to confuse his young sons.

If Cooper ever had a child, he'd make sure that kid knew he or she was loved beyond belief every day of his life.

For a moment he glanced at Leigh, wondering what it'd be like to have a child with her? His hair was dark. Would the child have black hair, or lighter hair like Leigh? Would his eyes be a warm chocolate brown?

Ruthlessly bringing his wayward thoughts under control, he listened to her chatter about the differences in apartments and wished she would stop talking about moving away. Her aunt and uncle wouldn't be returning home for another two months. She should stay and housesit. There'd be time enough after Lila and Paul returned for Leigh to find a place of her own.

When they finished eating, Cooper drove back to the office so Leigh could pick up her car. He followed her to Willow Creek.

Leigh parked in the back of the Porters' house. Shutting the car door, she waited. Should she wave good-night? Or wait to see if he wanted to continue the evening. Slowly, she crossed the grass toward Cooper. She didn't want the evening to end just yet.

"Come in for a nightcap?" he asked as she approached.

"I'd like that."

She hadn't been inside his house since they'd been teenagers. Curious to see what it looked like, she followed him through the back door.

The kitchen was tidy, though rather plain. He poured them each a small snifter of brandy and motioned to Leigh.

"Go on through to the front. We can sit on the porch if you like."

The hallway leading from the back to front was plain. Leigh wondered if the entire house was this way, or if Cooper had his stamp on certain rooms. A peek into the living room as they passed convinced her he didn't spend a lot of time decorating.

"Where are your pictures?" she asked, sitting on one of the chairs that lined the front of the house.

"I don't have many. Samuel doesn't send pictures. My Dad would never get before a camera."

For the first time since she'd known him, Leigh felt sorry for Cooper Bryant. The man who seemed so in charge of his life and destiny now seemed lonely and alone.

Her heart ached to provide him all he needed. But she wisely kept her thoughts to herself. If he wanted something different, he'd go after it. Of that she had no doubts. But he'd missed a woman's touch growing up. Still did, it appeared.

"What are you going to do about an apartment?" he asked.

"Keep looking I guess."

"Saturday?"

"What?"

"I could go with you on Saturday."

"No, thanks. I think I'm better doing it on my own," she said with a teasing smile. "You intimidate the managers."

"Only that old lady who thought we were looking at it for ourselves."

"A natural mistake when two people look at a place together."

"Maybe. Stay here until your aunt returns."

"Why?"

"Why not?"

"Is that the lawyer's way of avoiding explaining?"

Cooper reached out and lazily pulled her from her chair into his lap. Leigh went willingly, carefully setting her brandy snifter on the railing and leaning against his hard chest. He'd taken off his suit jacket, removed his tie and loosened the top buttons of his shirt. Wrapped in his arms, she could felt the heat radiating from his strong body.

"I want you, Leigh," Cooper said before his mouth met hers.

His lips were warm and firm as he moved to deepen the kiss.

Leigh answered his kiss with one of her own. If this had happened eleven years ago she'd have been in heaven.

Now she was wiser. At least she hoped so.

But it still felt like heaven. She reveled in the sensations that rushed through her. His hands moved against her arms, fingers threaded in her hair.

Sanity resurfaced and she pulled back. Danger loomed over her like the sword of Damocles. She'd loved this man years ago and he'd spurned her. Was she crazy to allow herself to draw closer now?

Pushing herself away from Cooper was the hardest thing she'd ever done, but she had to.

"I have to go," she said, breathlessly.

"Don't go, Leigh. Stay with me."

"I can't."

She all but ran to the safe haven of her aunt's house. Cooper's voice called her, but she didn't pause a step. Only after the kitchen door was firmly shut and locked behind her did Leigh draw a deep breath.

It had happened. Despite all her efforts, all her good intentions, she'd fallen in love with Cooper Bryant.

"Oh, nooo," she wailed.

She had thought herself immune to the man but she craved him like an addiction. She loved him just the way he was. Like Megan and her Frederick. Cooper annoyed her sometimes, but she'd never change a thing about him. If he'd only come to care for her.

But she knew that was a foolish dream. One she'd thought she'd outgrown. Obviously not.

Too upset to even think, she grabbed the journal like a lifeline. She'd started jotting down the different ideas to give to Meredith. Quickly she reviewed the list, tucking the paper in the front of the journal. Tonight her emotions wouldn't allow her to think through the list.

She'd read to see what Megan did next. The longing to skip ahead to see if Megan and Frederick had married was strong.

But for some reason Leigh wanted to watch the relationship unfold as it had happened. She'd find out soon enough. For a moment, she fervently hoped that Megan had found all the happiness she wanted with Frederick.

Today is the last of the spring cleaning. We're doing the parlor. First we had to wash the curtains. They are so heavy when wet and wringing them out takes Mama and me working together. The boys dragged the rug to the line in the back and spent the afternoon beating the dirt from it. As I dust and rearrange the things on the marble table, I took special note of the different items. Daddy's pipe is always waiting for him. The derreotype is old and I carefully cleaned it, asking Mama where it came from. Her smile is secretive, her eyes distant. Your father and I bought that together long ago, she told me. She looked around the room and smiled. Most of the things here we bought together, she said.

It's a wonderful thing to make a home with another person, Mama told me. To find what is special to you both, and then keep it where you can touch it, enjoy it, remember the happy days when you obtained it. A home should be restful and serene. A safe place for everyone to return to at day's end. Especially for a man. He's been out in the world all day fighting to make a living that will suit him and his family. The last thing he needs when he returns home is chaos.

I wonder if Frederick and I will build a home together? Will we have furniture and decorative items that will hold special meaning for us? Make home a calm and serene place so a man can rest when he is there, Mama said. It is advice I must always remember. Strive to fill his life with little things that show I care. Mama and Daddy have the derreotype and the other things in the parlor and their bedroom. What will Frederick and I have?

Leigh closed the journal and dreamily gazed off into space. She could make Cooper's house a real home. Fill it with color and pictures and paintings, with love and laughter and genuine caring. Show him he need not live like his father, cut off from the special touches that make home a wonderful special place.

If she ever got the chance.

Which she wouldn't.

Sighing softly, Leigh closed the journal and tried to go to sleep. But the memory of Cooper's lips on hers refused to fade. She wished she'd stayed for more.

Chapter Nine

The parlor is spotless. And it gave me a good feeling when I entered to greet Frederick when he came over last night. Mama and Daddy sat with us for a while. Then they permitted us to sit on the porch alone. Frederick told me about his day and I told him what I had done. For a moment I felt like we were truly connected in a way strangely different from anyone else on earth.

Then he spoiled everything. He said he'd heard something about me that was displeasing. Without thinking, I flared up and before I could say spit, he was angry. He had the audacity to lecture me as if I were still a child. I turned eighteen months ago. I am a woman full grown and his saying I was childish was the last straw. I stood up and told him what I thought.

We were too loud. Mama rushed out on the porch to see what was going on. Frowning at me, she cordially bid Frederick good evening. Then she sat with me and asked what had happened. When I explained, still so furious I wanted to stamp my foot, she nodded and took my hands. Megan, she said, there will be many difficulties in life's road. But a soft word turns away wrath. Never forget that.

I tried to defend myself. His accusations were false. She smiled and nodded, telling me she suspected as much. Another thing to always remember is you can catch more flies with honey than vinegar. Be your sweet self and he will come around.

Mothers can be trying at times. I wanted her to stand up for me, vilify his name. Instead, she gives me another old saying.

Yet, there is some merit in it I can see now that I've calmed down. Maybe I reacted too swiftly.

I shall bake him some cookies and take them round this afternoon. I'm sure Mama will say that is proper. And I will go as far as apologizing for my temper. But not for anything else. If he can't accept that, he's not the man for me.

Leigh jotted another line or two on her list and closed her eyes. The sun felt good against her skin. The dark glasses sheltered her from its harsh glare. The warmth made her sleepy. She had to watch the time. Cooper would be home soon and she didn't want to be in the yard sunbathing when he returned.

Her discovery last night that she still loved the man continued to worry her. She dare not let him suspect.

For now the afternoon was perfect. She floated in that state between full sleep and awareness. She heard the hum of bees in the patch of clover that grew near the back of the yard. The birds were silent—probably napping, she thought idly.

Had Megan and Frederick patched things up? Had Megan applied her mother's philosophy and been sweet to Frederick? Could Leigh be sweet to a man who made her angry?

Probably not. She'd want to knock his head off. Yet people could be angry at each other and not end their relationship. Everyone got mad sometimes.

She wished again that she'd known Megan. Wished they had grown up together and exchanged girlish confidences. Wished she could have discussed the different steps she took with her. Were they really the way to a man's heart? Or only the foolish imagination of a young woman at the beginning of the last century?

Of course, she'd had Meredith to exchange confidences with

as a girl and that had been great. Her cousin was special. Which nudged her further. She still needed to finish her list to give to Meredith. She was curious to find out if Megan's ideas truly worked.

She'd insist her cousin try them, just as Megan had listed them. In a minute she'd read some more of the journal and write any new points down. In a minute…

Slowly Leigh drifted to sleep.

"I don't think Sleeping Beauty fell asleep in the sun," a familiar voice said softly in her ear. "She might have gotten a case of terminal sunburn."

Leigh awoke with a start. Opening her eyes, she looked into Cooper's deep gaze.

"You'll get burned."

"It's late, the rays aren't so strong now," she said, her tongue scarcely able to form the words.

Cooper was here, a mere few inches away. Her heart pounded. Would he kiss her again? Like last night's kiss? And if so could she keep any semblance of normality or would he guess instantly that she had fallen in love again? Or, had she ever lost the love she felt for him?

Had she ever stopped? Had she just damped down her emotions until she thought she had recovered from lovesickness? He'd been the standard against which she'd measured every man she'd dated. The others had all fallen short.

"You can still burn. What are you reading?"

"My great-grandmother's journal. I told you about it the other night," she said, gripping it tightly.

"Interesting?"

"Yes."

Blinking in the bright sunshine, she tried to see him clearly.

He was back-lighted from the sun, his face in shadow.

"Is it late, is that why you're home?" she asked still a bit confused from her nap.

"I took off a little early. Want to have dinner together? I could throw some hamburgers on a grill."

Leigh swallowed, remembering all the admonitions in the journal. But for once she didn't give a thought to playing hard to get. Sometimes a woman needed to grasp an opportunity.

"Yes, I'd like that. I can bring a salad."

"Come over when you're ready. I'm going in to change."

Ten minutes later Leigh carried a large bowl through the backyard and knocked on his screen door.

"Come on in," Cooper called.

Entering, she took a deep breath. She was determined to enjoy the time spent together and not let him suspect a thing. She'd be friendly, polite and follow Megan's advice to the letter.

And memorize every moment spent with Cooper.

"I'll fire up the grill in the back. When the coals are ready, we'll cook these," Cooper said, forming patties from ground meat.

Leigh nodded, letting her gaze follow the long length of his muscular legs showing beneath the shorts he wore. The white T-shirt outlined his muscular shoulders and back. Taking a deep breath, she repeated her vow to remain friendly, not lovestruck like the teenager she'd once been.

"I'll put this in the refrigerator," Leigh said crossing to the large unit.

Once done, she turned to walk back to stand beside Cooper. How often had she longed for similar evenings so long ago? The two of them, together, preparing a meal?

"Can I help with anything else?"

"I don't think so. It's not a very elaborate meal."

"I don't need elaborate."

Leaning against the counter, Leigh watched as he worked.

"How was court?" she asked.

"Went well. I think we'll do summations tomorrow and send it to the jury."

"Will they work over the weekend?"

"No, probably begin their deliberations on Monday. It's not a sequestered jury."

"And do you think you'll win?"

He smiled grimly.

"Yes, but it's been a tough case. And I got blindsided at the onset by my client not telling me the full truth."

"How did you know?"

Cooper glanced at her as if to see if she really wanted him to continue. Seeing the interest on her face, he related as much as he could about the case without violating attorney-client privilege.

Leigh listened attentively. Cooper's work fascinated her. Cooper fascinated her.

The sun was still warm when they moved to the grill. Leigh asked more question about the different cases Cooper worked on and he answered them all. Soon the sizzling burgers were ready. Buns had been toasted and the salad brought out.

"I didn't bring any dressing, don't you have any?" Leigh asked, peering into the refrigerator.

"No. I'll run next door and get it. Does Lila keep it in the refrigerator door?"

"Yes, but I can go," she said. "I'm the one who forgot to bring any."

"No trouble. What do you want?"

"Ranch."

Leigh spread mustard on her bun, piled pickles on and then

looked for the onions. Hesitating only a moment, she loaded them on the bun. She loved them. And if she kept her wits about her tonight, she wouldn't have to worry about her breath. She planned to stay out of arm's reach of Cooper.

Where was the man? She looked out the window. Couldn't he find the dressing? She was sure she'd put it right in the tray in the door. Pushing open his screen door, she walked across to her aunt's house.

"Can't you find—"

She stopped suddenly in the doorway, her heart freezing. Cooper held the journal in one hand, the list for Meredith in the other. She hadn't had a chance to give it to her cousin yet. She had just added the last bit, about the honey and vinegar.

His face appeared carved from stone.

"What is this?"

His voice sounded cold as ice. His eyes flint hard.

Unable to move, Leigh stared at him, at a total loss for words. She'd left the journal on the counter. Why had he picked it up? The list had been tucked inside, she was sure of it.

Why couldn't she have taken it back upstairs? Clearing her voice, she drew a deep breath.

"My great-grandmother's journal," she said.

"And this?"

He held the list by the corner as if it might contaminate him.

"Just a list," she said.

Her heart raced. Panicked, she didn't know what to do. She wanted to snatch it from his hands, ball it up and throw it away. But she remained where she was, staring at him, unable to move an inch.

"'*Get him talking about himself.*' You did that one well. I hope you weren't too bored."

"I can explain," she tried, "It's for Meredith."

"The list's for *Meredith?*" Cooper said incredulously. "For *you,* I'd say. '*The way to a man's heart is through his stomach—fix something really delicious that he likes—like cake.*' Another one you did well."

Cooper gave her no chance to speak.

Her heart sank. He was furious. And the cold control he held over that anger made it seem even stronger. She wanted to say something, but she couldn't. Regret slammed through her. Would he listen to her? Or would he jump to conclusions? Conclusions that would be all too close to the truth?

"'*Catch flies with honey?*' Is that supposed to be me? A fly?"

He slammed the journal down on the table and advanced toward her, his eyes dark with anger.

"It's not what you think," she said, mesmerized by his tone. Would he give her a chance to explain? Attempt to understand?

"I think it is. I think you have practiced every one of the things on this stupid list with me. '*Do the unexpected*'—like a kidnap picnic? '*Wear pretty dresses?*' You've done that to a fare-thee-well. '*Practice being feminine.*' Do you have to practice that, Leigh? I thought that came naturally. But then I thought everything about you lately was natural. I didn't realize it was a part of a big plan to capture my attention. What were you after? Marriage? After all these years, have you forgotten what I said last time? That I don't want you. I don't love you and I sure don't plan to be a part of your stupid convoluted plans to land yourself a husband. Go back to New York. Maybe things like this work with men back in your great grandmother's day, but they sure don't here!"

His anger seemed to shimmer in the air. Leigh held her ground. she knew Cooper would never lose control no matter how irate he became. Frantically she sought the words that would quench his fury.

Crumbling the page into a tight ball, he threw it on the floor and stormed out.

"I guess this means dinner's off," Leigh said softly, still staring straight ahead.

The pain began in her heart and spread until she was almost shaking. Tears filled her eyes, but she blinked quickly to dispel them. It was no more than she deserved. And no more than she expected. He'd never had a use for her. Nothing had really changed. Except for a few weeks, she'd let herself believe there might be a chance. He'd been attentive, loving, romantic.

And it all meant nothing.

Slowly, she reached out for the journal and carried it upstairs. Her appetite gone, she didn't want dinner. She didn't want anything except oblivion to the pain that gripped her. She couldn't even read about Megan and Frederick.

Was it coincidence or prophesy that told of Megan's and Frederick's fight right before her fight with Cooper? Had the entire sequence of events been tied somehow to the past, like an endless loop that played over and over with each generation?

She didn't care. Falling into bed, she gazed dry-eyed at the ceiling, clutching the journal to her.

Truth be told, she'd been happier than ever these last few weeks. Without a job, unsure what she would do with her future, it hadn't mattered. She'd been so caught up in Cooper the rest had faded to insignificance.

More fool her.

She had known intellectually as soon as she'd seen him when she arrived that nothing had changed. But her heart refused to believe it. Maybe now it would.

Cooper stormed across the yard. Glancing at the table set for two it was all he could do to refrain from tipping it over and sending the food and utensils sliding off onto the grass. He yanked open the screen door and stepped inside. Her scent still lingered in the air. He drew a deep breath, imprinting it forever.

He'd thought things were different this time. He was supposed to be the clever hotshot attorney. Yet he'd fallen for her routine like a raw law clerk on his first case. She'd been much more sophisticated in her pursuit this time. Of course she'd had years to perfect her technique. It seemed so smooth.

Clenching his hands into hard fists, Cooper paced the kitchen remembering that blasted list and how Leigh had played him like a first-class idiot. She'd been so attentive when he spoke about work. He'd thought she had been genuinely interested. He'd actually reveled in sharing his thoughts about the cases with her. Had been proud of her interest.

And it was all fake.

He leaned on the sink and looked out the window, across to her house. He wanted to go back and yell at her, to rant and rave about the shameful way she'd deliberately enticed him. Flaunting her long legs in those dresses, making him want her like he hadn't wanted anyone in years. Rail at her for the shameful way she captivated his interest, and his heart, when it had been nothing but a challenge to her. A game.

His heart?

"No, never that," he said firmly.

Pushing away, he went to the cabinet and found the whisky. Pouring himself a glass, he went through to his study, on the opposite side of the house from Leigh's. He refused to even glance her way accidentally. Not tonight, not ever again.

Nursing his drink, Cooper gazed out the window, his mind churning with raw fury—and hot memories.

Friday morning Leigh rose early. She'd spent a miserable

night. Nightmares had plagued her. She'd been running after Cooper and every time he disappeared.

"No need to be an expert to know what that means," she grumbled as she stood beneath the hot shower. "How can a woman be so stupid? I wonder if it's genetic?"

Drawing one of her new dresses from the closet, she hesitated a long moment. Then defiantly put it on. She liked wearing the dresses. Once she had a new job, she might have to resume her suits but she could please herself until then.

She ate a hasty breakfast, toast and tea. Then tackled her resumé. Sending emails to a dozen firms, she included the final resume. By next week she should start hearing something.

And in the meantime, she'd continue to look for a place to live. The sooner she moved away from Cooper's proximity the better for her sanity.

After driving to the apartment complex on Rose Street later that day, she was disappointed to discover the apartment had been rented. It was the one she'd liked the best.

"But, it wasn't good enough for Cooper. I should have acted on my own impues," she said to herself as she got back into her car.

The rest of the afternoon she spent looking at places. The one on Coldridge was almost as nice as the first one she'd liked. But it was nearer the train tracks and might prove to be noisy. Telling the manager she'd be in touch, she headed for Willow Creek.

On impulse she checked her watch, then drove to Meredith's.

"Hey," Meredith greeted her when she rang the bell.

"Doing anything tonight?" Leigh asked as she entered her cousin's apartment.

For a moment she gazed around. Maybe she should see about an apartment in this complex. It wasn't that far to Charlotte, and she'd be close to Meredith.

"Nope, what's up? You look like you lost your best friend."

It was unexpected. Leigh would have sworn she'd never do such a thing. But at her cousin's words, she burst into tears.

Startled, Meredith crossed over to her and hugged her tightly.

"Oh, Leigh, what's wrong?"

Rubbing her eyes, trying desperately to stem the tears, Leigh sniffed and shook her head.

"Delayed reaction, I guess."

"To losing your job?"

Meredith patted her shoulder, looking into her tear-drenched eyes.

"I guess."

She looked for a tissue, saw a napkin on the table and used that. Taking a shaky breath she tried to smile at her cousin, but it was more than she could do.

"I blew it big-time."

"Your job?"

Leigh shook her head. "Cooper."

"Cooper?" Meredith sat on the arm of the sofa and looked puzzled. "I don't get it."

Leigh drew a deep breath and sank on the sofa. Opening her purse, she withdrew the crumbled sheet and held it out for Meredith.

"Remember I told you about Megan's advice?"

Meredith nodded and reached for the paper.

"I wrote down the different suggestions to show you. I wanted you to try them to see if they really worked or if it had been some kind of weird reaction that made Cooper seem interested in me when I tried Megan's ideas."

"And?"

Meredith scanned the list.

"Cooper found the journal and the list and now he thinks I was playing at getting him to be interested in me. Like I did when I was a teenager. He's furious."

Shrewdly Meredith studied her cousin.

"And that matters?"

Nodding her head, Leigh blotted her eyes again.

"I love him, Meredith. I did when I was a teenager and I still do. I managed to build a life in New York. I was reasonably happy there. But no man ever appealed to me like Cooper. And now I know why. He's the man I love. I guess I will always love him. What a depressing thought."

"Only if he doesn't love you back."

"He doesn't. He's always been up-front and honest about that. He has no use for women, except as a casual date from time to time, I guess. Why can't I get that hammered home in my brain?"

"Sometimes I think the brain and heart never talk to one another. Don't you think I could make better choices if I'd think things through?" her cousin said dryly. "I'm sorry, Leigh. I know you're hurt. But honey, I really think you should have had better sense. Cooper won't ever change. And you can't live your whole life pining for a man who doesn't want you."

"I know."

Meredith looked at the list again, her face slowly smiling.

"Tell me more about this list. I'm intrigued."

Leigh explained the different points as Megan had written them down. She enjoyed telling Meredith about the ins and outs of Megan's courting.

"I still think they got together. I can't believe you didn't read the diary in detail."

"Never had the time. When you're finished, I'll read it through."

Thoughtfully Meredith tapped her finger against the sheet.

"I've been trying to be a modren woman. I'm comfortable calling a man to ask him out. Isn't this a bit old-fashioned?"

"Maybe, but there's a lot of truth in her notes. If you ask a man out, and he goes, you've become the hunter. Men like to do the hunting bit. At least when he asks you out, you know he wants it."

"It makes me feel like a squirrel."

Leigh shook her head.

"Not really. It's more of doing what feels comfortable and seeing what happens. Try it. Just be yourself, but rein in some of your more assertive tendencies. I tried each one. Some without even knowing that I was doing it."

Meredith nodded thoughtfully.

"Okay, Leigh. If you can do this, I can, too."

"It may not work. It sure backfired with me. But I still think her suggestions are worthwhile. And I liked doing things this way. It felt natural and fun. Wearing dresses for a while is a change I like. I find I flirt just a bit more—even with the bag boy at the grocery store. I feel I move a bit more femininely when I walk. It gives me a great feeling."

"Shorts and pants are so convenient."

"Dresses are fun, and feminine. Try it for a month and see what happens."

"Are you going to?"

"What?" Leigh looked at her cousin.

"Are you going to continue with this?"

"I don't know, why?"

"I heard that you've had several calls from Karl and from

Peter Jordan. You've put them off long enough, why not say yes next time?"

"Oh, Karl is so predictable. And Peter—"

"But if you're sincere about moving on, you have to forget about Cooper and try spending time with others," Meredith said gently.

"You're right." Leigh sighed. Life was difficult sometimes.

Leigh spent Friday night and all day Saturday with her cousin. When Meredith was tempted to phone Josiah, Leigh challenged her again to follow Megan's suggestions.

When Meredith hesitated, Leigh offered a pact. They'd both practice Megan's ideas for one month and then take stock of where they stood. And Leigh agreed to go out with whomever asked her to give herself a chance with someone besides Cooper.

But, she would not take last-minute dates.

Late Saturday afternoon she returned home. Ignoring the house next door, she quickly drove to the back and hurried into her own house. She had the rest of the journal to finish. She wanted to know what happened with Megan and Frederick. Were there other suggestions her great-grandma could offer?

The phone rang and her heart lifted.

"Hello?"

"Hi, Leigh, Karl here. I thought I'd see if you're free tomorrow."

His voice was hesitant. For a moment Leigh almost refused to see him, then her common sense kicked in. She'd do better going out with Karl than brooding at home. And she and Meredith had made a pact.

"I am, what did you have in mind, Karl?"

"That's great. I thought we could play some tennis at the country club in the afternoon and then maybe stay for dinner.

They have a swell buffet."

For a moment the memory of another Sunday night at the country club flooded Leigh. She blinked.

This was a chance to overwrite those memories with newer ones. Trying to put some enthusiasm in her voice, Leigh accepted.

As soon as she hung up, she wished she could call Karl back and cancel. How could she go out with another man when Cooper held her heart?

Yet, if she didn't, she'd be condemning herself to many lonely hours. Cooper made it clear he wasn't interested. In fact, she'd be surprised if he didn't despise her after this.

Taking the stairs two at a time, she hurried up to her room to fetch the journal. The sooner she finished the book, the sooner she'd know what happened to her great-grandmother. If she hadn't been pacing herself while reading it, and dreaming about what could never be, she'd have finished days ago.

Her date with Karl was pleasant, Leigh thought when she went to bed Sunday night. Nothing earth-shattering, but it'd been fun to play tennis again. And she'd been reacquainted with several other citizens of Willow Creek. It'd certainly been better than staying home alone all day.

Monday she received a call from a company which had received her resumé. And a call from Karl inviting her out on Wednesday night. Then Peter Jordan called. He'd been one of the men to stop by their table Sunday night and he wanted to know if she were free on Friday evening.

Leigh said yes to the interview, to Karl and to Peter. Maybe she couldn't have the man of her dreams, but it wouldn't hurt to show him just because he didn't want her, others didn't feel the same way.

Leigh's interview was Tuesday morning. Leigh loved the prospects of the job. It sounded exciting and offered more potential than she expected. She met several different people during her interview—from the man who'd be her immediate boss to the president of the firm. When they offered to take her to lunch, she was sure she'd have the position if she wanted.

The offer came later that afternoon. Thrilled at finding something so soon after losing her job in New York, she quickly accepted. Agreeing to start in two weeks, she planned to use the intervening days in finding a place to stay and return to New York to pack and move.

She longed to share her good news with Cooper, but prudently avoided him. She hadn't seen him since he'd stormed out of the kitchen Thursday night. And she'd do her level best to avoid him until she moved, maybe even beyond.

Rubbing her chest, over her heart, she tried to ease the ache that seemed a permanent affliction. No use crying over spilt milk, as her great-grandma Megan had written.

She and Meredith celebrated her new job Tuesday night. Karl was delighted with her news and insisted on champagne at their dinner on Wednesday. By the time she had dinner with Peter, she'd located the perfect apartment and put down a deposit.

Her flight was due to leave early Saturday morning. She planned to spend several days in New York, wind up her affairs there, and arrange for movers to come for her furniture. When she returned to North Carolina, she'd move straight into her new place.

Meredith understood why she couldn't stay in Aunt Lila's house. And if the yard needed more work soon, she'd hire someone.

It was late when Peter brought her home Friday. They'd gone dancing in Charlotte and Leigh tried to make the evening as enjoyable for her date as she could. He was an interesting man, charming and funny. She enjoyed herself. And she knew he was interested in her when he tried to press for another date. She explained she would be tied up for a couple of weeks. She promised to call him as soon as she returned and got settled in her new apartment.

Slowly Leigh packed her clothes. She planned to drive to Meredith's in the morning to have her cousin take her to the airport. Since she didn't plan to return to her aunt's house, she made sure she had all her things.

Inevitably she was drawn to the window that overlooked Cooper's house. For a long moment she stared at it, her heart aching with loss. She'd been so happy these several weeks. Smiling sadly she remembered every hour spent together. She'd miss him. Miss what they might have had.

But it was time to move on. The whole world was waiting for her and she couldn't stay in the one spot much as she longed to.

She had practice in this. Eleven years ago she'd had to move on. Now she knew she could succeed. Life might not be as wonderful alone, but there were joys to be found along the way.

And maybe she fall for another man some day.

"Goodbye, my love," she said softly, pressing her hand against the glass as if she could reach across the yards and touch his home. Touch him.

Chapter Ten

Cooper leaned again his porch railing and watched as Peter walked Leigh up to her door. He'd glance at his watch, but didn't want to make any move that might draw their attention. He knew it was late. He'd been sitting out here for hours.

When he'd seen Peter pick her up, he'd been curious. She'd been out three times since Thursday night. He wondered if she were practicing her feminine wiles on all the men in Willow Creek as she had with him.

Anger roiled inside. He wanted to purge the sensations that wouldn't turn loose, but not at the cost of seeing her again.

She'd proved as shallow as Celia. Each out for her own gain. Never mind how the man felt.

For a long moment he tried to recapture the anguish he'd felt when Celia had thrown him over. There was nothing. Except a certain nostalgia for the young man who had thought himself in love for the first time.

Looking back now, he should have spotted the inconsistencies. She'd never declared her undying love. He'd projected his own feelings onto her. He'd wanted her and had been out to prove something. What, all these years later, he wasn't sure.

His anger tightened toward Leigh. She'd deliberately sought

him out this visit. Planned her campaign like a general. He'd thought she'd changed, but she'd just become more crafty.

Really? An insidious voice inside whispered. *Really?*

Who called her to ask her out? Pushing until she agreed?

Had she even asked him for anything? Only the one night when she said Meredith and Josiah were also coming to dinner.

Other than that, he'd done all the asking. Done all the pursuing.

He tightened his fists. What was Peter doing? If he was kissing her, Cooper had half a mind to wander across the lawn and stop it. A quick sock on his jaw should do nicely to put the man in his place and assuage some of Cooper's anger.

Almost growling with disgust, he shifted his eyes away from the house next door and tried to erase the images that danced before him, of Leigh with her arms around Peter. Her soft body pressed against the other man's. Leigh's sweet mouth moving against Peter's. Cooper tried to hold on to his anger, build the wall higher around his heart. Blast it all, he was not going to have anything further to do with her.

His gaze focused on the Bandeleys' house. He'd seen the elderly couple just that morning. Mr. Bandeley had mowed their front lawn. Mrs. Bandeley had come out right afterwards with a large glass of lemonade. They'd talked softly and laughed.

Cooper had looked away when Mr. Bandeley had leaned over to kiss his wife of forty-two years.

His gaze moving, he looked at the Foresters' home. They'd been married a long time, lived on the street their entire marriage. All their children were grown. He'd heard a few weeks ago that their eldest son and his wife were expecting a baby.

Lila and Paul would love for Meredith to marry and give them a grandchild. He was sure Leigh's parents would love it as well.

He wondered for a moment if his father ever thought about grandchildren.

Peter walked down the sidewalk to his car. Cooper watched, his eyes narrowed. Took the man long enough to tell her good-night, he fumed. Not that he cared what Leigh did, or with whom. But Cooper didn't move from that spot on the porch until the house next door was completely dark. In the morning, he'd return her salad bowl from the ill-fated dinner they never ate. See if she wanted to apologize. See how she looked. See—

He shook his head in disgust, letting his gaze travel along the length of the street. Every family there except his had remained a family unit. Each husband and wife still greeted each other with affection, caring, and love. Grown children came back to visit, laughing and hugging their parents upon arrival.

Leigh had been right about one thing. His family had been the exception on this street. And he finally admitted he didn't know the entire story. Only the part a young seven-year-old put together when he never saw his mother again. When his father had changed to the embittered man he was still.

What had gone wrong? Could it have been avoided? Wasn't love enough?

Leigh hugged her cousin and smiled.

Thanks again for the lift. I'll see you in a week or so."

Sun streamed in the high airport windows, dazzling in the early morning sky. The concourse wasn't crowded except around the screening area.

Meredith nodded, yawning.

"I wouldn't get up this early on a Saturday for just anyone," she said with a mock grumble.

"I appreciate it. Take care of yourself. And remember our pledge."

"As if you'd let me forget. Where's the journal?"

"I left it by my bed. I still have some left to read. But I knew you'd have more time to read it this week than I will. Take it if you want. I'll finish it when I get back. Bye."

Soon airborne, Leigh relaxed against her seat back. She had a million things to do in New York. Some favorite places she wanted to see one last time, friends she had to tell goodbye, and her apartment to pack.

When she returned to North Carolina, it wouldn't be to the arms of a tall, dark, gorgeous man, but to a new job, a new apartment and a new start in life.

She wished she could have finished the journal, but she hadn't. The last passage she read stayed with her, though, as the plane flew north.

My grandmother Witherspoon came today for Sunday dinner. She is a real tartar. I've been afraid of her most of my life. But today she asked to speak to me alone. I thought for sure I'd done something wrong, but she just wanted to congratulate me on reaching eighteen. She gave me a lovely lace handkerchief that she said she'd made as a young girl. Then she looked at me sternly with those dark eyes that seem to see everything and said, remember what the Good Book says, Megan: Now abide faith hope and love, these three, but the greatest of these is love. Faith that all you need to know in life your parents have taught you. Remember those lessons, girl.

Hope for the future. It will be what you make of it. There will be hard times, too, but don't give up on hope. And love, child. I hope your life will be enriched with all the love your heart can hold. Now tell me about this Frederick I hear so much about!

I almost cried, she was so sweet. I'll never be afraid of her again.

I told her about the fight we had, and how I had gone with cookies to talk with him. How when I explained what had truly happened he was so quick to apologize and ask my forgiveness. Of course I didn't tell her of his kiss. That is just between us. I know I love him and told him so. He loves me and will be speaking to Papa this week.

Leigh wished telling Cooper she loved him would convince him that they should be together. She had faith in herself, however. In knowing she had done all she could to show the man she truly cared. While she had practiced some of the suggestions laid down by her great-grandmother, none had been artificial. Just a slower, old-fashioned courtship. Wryly she wondered how she ever could have explained that to Cooper.

Her hope came for a brighter future. She'd loved and not been loved in return. But that didn't change her feelings. She'd go on and do her best to find another love to share her life. She'd keep the faith and hope in a lasting love like the one that came to her great-grandparents, to her own parents, to most of the families she knew.

And for now, she had plenty to do to pack up and leave New York. One chapter of her life was ending. She was excited about the next chapter.

Cooper frowned impatiently. Where was the woman? Her car had been gone when he rose this morning. It was now late afternoon and she still hadn't returned. He looked out the side window for the millionth time.

Meredith turned her car into the driveway and headed to the back.

Grabbing the bowl, he quickly crossed the backyard. Knocking on the kitchen door, he waited impatiently the few moments it took until Meredith appeared.

"Hello, Cooper."

Her tone was cool. She didn't invite him inside.

"Meredith. I'm returning a bowl. Where's Leigh?"

"New York by now," she said, opening the screen wide

enough to reach for the empty bowl.

Cooper went still.

New York?"

For a moment he wondered if his heart had stopped beating.

Meredith nodded, taking the bowl.

"Is this Mom's?"

"Yes. We had a salad."

They'd never eaten the salad. He'd thrown it out the next day.

Meredith nodded, waited.

"Was there something else?"

"I didn't know Leigh was returning to New York," he said slowly.

Meredith shrugged.

"I'm sure she thought you wouldn't care one way or the other. I have to leave now."

She stepped back to place the bowl on the counter, then stepped outside. She closed the door and locked it.

Cooper didn't move. Heading down the steps toward her car, she glanced over her shoulder at him. She carried the worn leather journal in her hand.

"You've got what you wanted, haven't you Cooper? No one and nothing to bother you? Or care about you? I can see you in another few years, as hard to deal with as your father. Don't worry about Leigh. She's young and pretty and has plenty going for her. She'll find a wonderful man who'll appreciate her for who she is and all the love she has to offer. I hope they have a dozen kids and are blissfully happy all their lives. The woman is a idiot who thinks she loves you. Goodbye, Cooper."

Meredith slammed her car door and raced her engine before backing swiftly from the driveway.

Cooper listened to the echo of her words. No one to care

about you. How much had Leigh *really* cared? Hadn't she been merely entertaining herself trying her tricks to get him to fall for her?

Or had she loved him? She'd followed him around as a teenager, tried to tell him years ago that she loved him, but he'd ruthlessly turned her away. He hadn't wanted some kid with a crush hanging around.

She'd come back.

But if he were honest, and Cooper was always honest, she hadn't pursued him. She'd all but ignored him until he asked to see her. Demanded to see her. Taken her dancing. Felt that sexy body press up against his. Kissed her until neither one of them could breathe.

The picnic had been fun. Discovering how she'd grown and matured had fascinated him. Listening to her talk about her job, about her friends in New York, had been enlightening. Looking for a place for her to live had been frustrating. She could stay at Lila's, her aunt wouldn't mind.

He missed her.

He looked north, as if he could see all the way to New York. He'd been ruthless a second time. And driven her away again. This time forever?

Had he been too hasty in condemning her because of some stupid list? She said she could explain, but he'd never given her the opportunity. What kind of fact finder did that make him? Why had he set himself up as judge and jury?

Four years was too long to live in one apartment, Leigh decided as she hauled another bag of trash to the basement. People ought to move every year to avoid accumulations of stuff that had no useful function. She was tired. This was the third trip today and she still had at least one more large bag of trash to haul down. Then she'd be finished sorting and could begin packing in earnest.

She stepped on the elevator and pushed the button for her floor. Tired as she felt, she had to keep going because the movers were due tomorrow and she had to make sure she didn't ship anything she no longer wanted. Money would be tight for a while and she couldn't afford the expense of recklessly shipping everything.

Stepping off the elevator, she reached into her pocket for her keys. The jeans she wore weren't very feminine, but necessary for cleaning and packing. Dresses would be in the way. But she missed them and looked forward to wearing her sun dresses again back in North Carolina.

"Leigh."

She stopped and looked up. Rubbing her eyes, she sighed. She was more tired than she thought. Now she was imagining things. If she could get through the rest of the sorting soon, she could get an early night, catch up on her sleep and be ready to go again tomorrow.

"Not talking?"

"Cooper?"

He wasn't a figment of her imagination? He was real?

"Last time I looked in the mirror," he said.

He wore jeans and a pullover shirt. The casual attire showed off his broad shoulders, rugged physique. She skimmed her gaze down his long legs. A small duffel bag lay at his feet.

"What are you doing here?"

Greedily Leigh looked at him, her heart thumping hard in her chest, her palms growing damp. She stepped closer until she felt the warmth from his body. Until she breathed in the scent of his aftershave. Her stomach dropped like a roller coaster and she just stared at him. The words of their last meeting echoed in her mind.

"I came to see you."

"In New York?"

"That's where you are. I went to your aunt's house on Saturday and Meredith told me you'd returned to New York."

"It's Tuesday," she said, trying to make sense of his being here.

"I had to make arrangements at the office yesterday. Are you going to invite me inside?"

Warily she watched him.

"Why?"

"I want to talk to you."

The stubborn set to his jaw warned her what he had to say probably wasn't good.

"About what?" she asked suspiciously.

"Inside?"

"Okay."

She stepped around him and unlocked her door. When she entered, she looked around at the shambles. She wished he'd seen the apartment when it had been tidy. It had been warm and welcoming and perfectly suited to her.

Now it looked as if a hurricane had blown through.

She raked her fingers through her hair. She hadn't put on any makeup that morning, just pulled on her jeans and top and set to work. So much for appearing feminine and ladylike. She crossed into the small living room and turned to watch Cooper.

He looked around the apartment and dropped his bag by the door. Shutting it, he leaned against it, his gaze moving to her.

"This is small. No wonder you thought the places in Charlotte were large."

She shrugged.

"Real estate's at a premium in Manhattan. I was lucky to be able to afford this place without having a roommate. Did you come all this way to see my apartment?"

"No, I came to see you."

His gray eyes gazed into hers. Even from across the width of the room, Leigh felt their impact. Swallowing hard she gestured to the sofa.

"Have a seat."

Say what you have to say and get out. How many times could she say goodbye?

Cooper lifted the stack of pictures leaning against the sofa and moved them out of the way.

"Housecleaning?"

Leigh shook her head and gingerly sat on the far edge of the sofa watching him cautiously.

"Packing up. I found a place and a job in Charlotte," she said.

"One we looked at?"

She shook her head.

He took a deep breath and looked around the room, then looked at her. Giving a halfhearted grin he tilted his head.

"I thought I'd practiced enough I could do this easily."

Frowning, Leigh stared at him.

"Do what?"

"Apologize first. I think I jumped to some erroneous conclusions the other night. But I've had a lot of time to think about things over the last week and I need to get everything squared away."

He fell silent and Leigh waited. Was she supposed to say something at this point?

"Like what?" she blurted out when she could stand the suspense no longer.

"When taking on a new client, or a new case, I make sure I know all the facts. I question, listen, analyze and get as complete a picture of the situation as I can. It never pays to jump to conclusions without knowing all the facts. But I did with you. And I think I owe it to both of us to remedy that."

"Cooper, you don't owe me anything. We had a few dates, shared some time together. You don't want to do that any more. End of discussion."

"Maybe you're jumping to conclusions," he said. "You look as if you're going to fall off the edge of the sofa."

Moving to sit more fully on the cushions, Leigh couldn't relax—too aware of Cooper's presence so close to her, of the scent of his aftershave which evoked deep memories of his kisses, the feel of his thick hair beneath her fingers, the sensations his lips brought when they brushed against hers, or nibbled against her neck or her cheek.

He moved until his knee pushed against her leg, one hand stretching out along the back until his fingers could brush her shoulder.

Resisting the urge to jump up and put the room between them, Leigh took a deep breath.

"What conclusions am I jumping to?" she asked, trying to concentrate on the conversation.

At a total loss as to why he really had come, she wished he'd get to the point before she did something really stupid like throw herself into his arms and beg he kiss her senseless.

"That I knew what I was saying."

"Huh?"

Startled, Leigh stared at him.

"Tell me about the diary and the list I read at your aunt's that night."

"There's not much to tell. Meredith and Aunt Lila found the journal when they cleaned out the attic last spring. It was written by my great-grandmother Megan when she turned eighteen. There is a lot of family information, she was a wonderful writer. And her handwriting's so clear it's easy to read." Leigh trailed off.

"And the list?"

Taking a deep breath, she looked at her fingers, twisting them in her lap.

"Megan was interested in a particular young man she knew and her aunts and mother were giving her hints on how to conduct herself as she and this young man got to know each other better. She called it her plan to find the perfect husband. I told Meredith and she wanted to know specifics about Megan's plan, so I copied down what I could remember."

Daring a glance at Cooper, she knew she had his full attention.

"So were you trying them out on me?"

"Sort of. But it started by accident. And if you had stopped to think about it, the list is innocuous. Really common-sense suggestions. I guess for Megan they were new and wonderful. But I'm a lot older than Megan was when she wrote that journal. And I've heard most of these suggestions before. Only I guess we forget the old ways sometimes in striving to be on the forefront of things."

"A plan for a husband? You're looking for a husband and thought why not give old Cooper Bryant a try?"

His voice was low, even. Was he mad?

"Not exactly. Actually you were my practice guy."

"Practice guy?" It was his turn to look startled. "What do you mean?"

"Well, if the suggestions worked with a hard case like you, they'd surely work with a different man if I found someone I wanted to marry."

"And it didn't worry you to toy with a man's affections?"

She laughed.

"You've never let anyone toy with you since you were a kid. And as cynical as you are about relationships and women, I knew there was no worry about hurting you."

Only herself when she was foolish enough to fall in love again.

"There you go jumping to conclusions again. You'd never make a good litigation attorney."

"Well, darn."

His hand slid down her arm and captured hers. Threading his fingers through hers, he rested their linked hands on his thigh.

Leigh's heart rate exploded, raced. What was Cooper doing?

"I'm glad you got a job in Charlotte," he said slowly, his thumb tracing random patterns on the back of her hand.

"You are? Why?"

"Makes it easier."

"Makes what easier?"

"Courting."

"Courting?"

Had she heard him correctly? Cooper talking about courting? Her?

"As you said, we're always in such a rush we seem to forget the old-fashioned way of doing things. Maybe that's what we need here."

"What we need here is some clarification of what you're talking about."

And quickly, before she lost all sense of reason. His thumb was driving her crazy, her heart was about to pound out of her chest and the impulse to scoot over and lean against the man was so strong she marveled she could resist.

"For a week I had to watch you go out with every guy in Willow Creek."

"Karl and Peter hardly comprise every guy in Willow Creek."

"Doesn't matter, seemed like it at the time."

"Oh?"

That raised interesting thoughts. Had Cooper been jealous?

"And while waiting for you to come home each night, I had plenty of time to think. To think and consider the interesting ideas you raised. Maybe there was more to my family breakup than I knew. Maybe my father played as big a part in it as my mother. And then I discovered it no longer mattered. I'm not my father and you are certainly not my mother."

Leigh blinked. She was getting confused again. What did his parents have to do with courting?

"Can you get to the courting part again?" she asked, her skin tingling from his touch, her internal temperature rising.

Cooper smiled and raised their linked hands, kissing the back of hers.

"I want to court you, Leigh."

He turned her hand over and kissed the pulse in her wrist.

"I want to marry you."

Releasing her hand, he placed a warm kiss in the palm.

"I want you to live with me forever and never leave."

Quizzically he looked at her.

The smile was tentative and melted her heart. His eyes were warm with love yet hesitant as if he was still unsure. How could the man ever doubt it for an instant?

Tears gathered and slipped over her cheeks.

"Don't cry," he exclaimed, drawing her into his arms and

hugging her tightly. "Don't cry, sweetheart. If you don't want to marry me, that's okay. No, it's not, but I'll learn to live with it. Leigh, don't be unhappy."

"Silly," she said against his neck, her arms creeping up to encircle him, hold him tightly against her as she closed her eyes and let the emotions flood through her.

"I love you, Cooper. I've loved you since I was fifteen years old. Through all the years, I've never stopped. I thought I could go on, but this summer sure made me question that. I love you so much!"

"I love you, Leigh. I can't say I've loved you since you were fifteen, but it's been a long time. Only I was too caught up in the idea that all women were like my mother. I couldn't bear to risk any chances."

"And now you don't feel like that?"

"Not like I used to. What I feel for you is strong, I'm willing to take a chance. It's better than living alone and imagining you with someone else, making love, having babies, and sharing your life. I want that all for myself. And if you think you've loved me all this time, I doubt you will up and leave."

"I'm never leaving!" she vowed, leaning back to gaze into his eyes.

But only for a second before his mouth came down on hers with a sweet kiss that immediately caused every other kiss to fade in comparison.

This was Cooper, the man she loved, the man who loved her back.

Leigh's heart was filled to overflowing. Together they'd put down roots so deep nothing could ever tear them out. And with their love, they'd find the happiness and delight in sharing their lives that others in her family had.

When the kiss ended, he looked into her eyes.

"So how long do I have to court you before I can ask you to be my wife?"

"I don't mind a really short courtship," she said softly.

"How short?"

"If we count all the time we've already spent together, I'd say we've done it," she said daringly.

Treasuring the look of love and devotion in his eyes, she wished she could capture the moment forever. But Leigh knew she'd never forget a single second of this day.

"I love you, Leigh Elizabeth Gaffney. Will you marry me?"

"I would be so honored to accept, Cooper Skylar Bryant. Thank you for asking me."

"Ever the proper old-fashioned girl," he said as he kissed her again.

They put through a call to Greece, sharing their happy news with Leigh's parents dispite the time difference. Then two more calls, first to Florida and then to California informed Cooper's father and brother.

eigh called Meredith next, excited to share her happiness.

"Wow, I thought one of the tenets from Great-grandma Megan was a leopard couldn't change his spots. What changed Cooper?" Meredith asked after extending her best wishes to her cousin.

"Love, I guess," Leigh answered, glowing with that emotion herself.

"Well your timing's great, I have just the wedding present for you."

"What's that?"

"Mom called yesterday and I asked her about the journal and Great-grandma Megan. She told me Megan and Frederick had fifty-two happy years together before he died. And where to find a copy of their photograph from their fiftieth anniversary party. I'll have it enlarged and give to you so you and Cooper will have something to live up to."

"It's nice to know how that story turned out. And to know mine will be the same."

"Sure, cousin?"

"As sure as love," Leigh said, reaching out to touch the man who would share her life

Maybe she should start her own journal. She could open with…*and the greatest of these is love.*

www.ingramcontent.com/pod-product-compliance
Lightning Source LLC
LaVergne TN
LVHW020718110826
845149LV00012B/2316

* 9 7 8 1 9 6 0 7 9 5 7 4 8 *